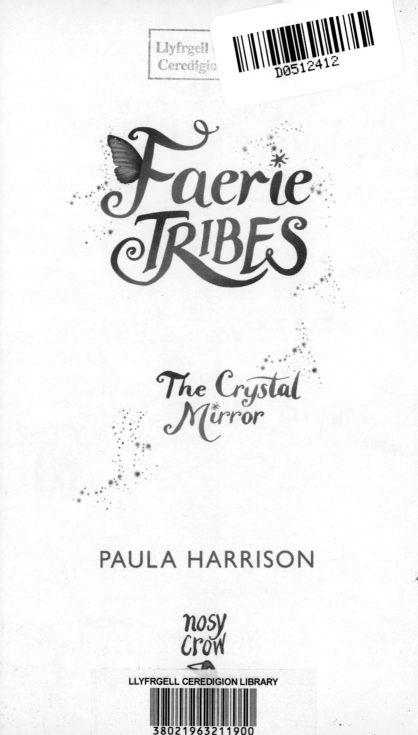

Faerie Tribes

The Crystal Mirror

PAULA HARRISON

nosy
crow

Skellmore and Surrounding Area

Mencladden Hill and Standing Stone

River Mistray

Faymere Lake

Hobbin Forest

Gillforth

HIGH STREET

to Pennington

(town)

Skellmore Farm

Faerie TRIBES

Farmland

Hairdressers

Mini Mart

Pet Shop

Silverbrook Close

Pond

Old Eagle Pub

Park

Church

The Cattery

Olowing Rise

Gnarlwood Lane

Skellmore Edge

For Abby, who opened these pages and flew with me

First published in the UK in 2013 by Nosy Crow Ltd
The Crow's Nest, 10a Lant Street
London, SE1 1QR, UK

Nosy Crow and associated logos are trademarks and/or registered
trademarks of Nosy Crow Ltd

1 3 5 7 9 10 8 6 4 2

A CIP catalogue record for this book is available from the British Library

Printed and bound in the UK by Clays Ltd, St Ives Plc
Typeset by Tiger Media Ltd, Bishops Stortford, Hertfordshire

Papers used by Nosy Crow are made from wood grown in
sustainable forests.

ISBN: 978 0 85763 201 2

www.nosycrow.com

Prologue

Ten years before

The child toddled down to the bottom of the garden and gazed at the grassy hill rising up on the other side of the gate. She looked through the bars and giggled. Black-winged figures flew over the top of the hill, outlined against the setting sun. They swooped and hovered as if they were dancing in the air. Spellbound, the little girl pulled at the latch and the gate creaked open.

A woman in a red dress ran down the path and scooped her up. "What are you doing out here, baby?"

The girl flapped her arms. "Fly, Mummy!"

The winged figures swooped even faster. A bright flash shot through the peaceful air and one of them crumpled before spiralling to the ground.

The woman ran inside, carrying the child with her, and locked the door. She set her daughter down gently and peered round the edge of the curtain, her face pale.

The little girl tugged at the hem of her mother's

skirt. Fine hair curled in wisps round her face. "Fly, Mummy?" she asked.

"Maybe one day, Laney." Her mother hugged her. "One day when we're far away from here."

CHAPTER
1

Laney opened her water bottle and took several big gulps. The water was warm and tasted sour like lemon juice. She lowered the bottle. For a second it looked as if the water was boiling, with big, fat bubbles rolling up to the surface. Then it was still.

Laney blinked. That was weird.

"Running round the track should be banned on the last day of term." Steph picked up her sports bag and stuffed her clothes into it. "Typical Miss Roderick, queen of PE torture."

Laney grinned and pushed back the fair hair that curled in wisps round her face. "Maybe they put that in her job description: *Must own a disgusting red tracksuit and enjoy making people suffer!*"

"They got exactly what they wanted then," said Steph.

The changing-room door banged as some of the other girls left.

Still thirsty, Laney decided to try another tiny swig of water to see how it tasted. As she tipped up the bottle, she caught a shadowy movement from the corner of her eye. The bottle was knocked out of her hand. Water splattered over her face and dripped down her clothes on to the changing-room floor.

"Oh, Laney!" said Jessie with mock sweetness. "Did I bump into you? I'm *so* sorry!"

Laney glared. "What did you do that for?" She

should have known it would be Jessie, and the gleam in the other girl's eyes showed exactly how sorry she was.

"It was just an accident." Jessie shook back her dark curls and flounced out of the changing room.

"Are you OK?" said Steph. "I don't know *what* is wrong with that girl."

"Don't worry about it. Jessie's been mean to me ever since nursery school. It's like part of her daily routine or something, and I didn't want that water anyway. It tasted really weird." Laney picked up the bottle. "I'm going to fill this up from the water fountain." She bent down to close her bag. At least her books had escaped getting wet.

As she straightened up she noticed Claudia watching her from across the changing room. As their eyes met, she gave Laney a half-smile and turned away to brush her hair.

Laney picked up her bag, staring curiously at Claudia, but the other girl didn't turn round again. Over the last few weeks she'd caught Claudia studying her a few times. She found it weird because Claudia was one of those cool types who'd never seemed to notice her before. She pushed through the changing-room door with Steph behind her. They walked down the corridor and through another set of doors to find Jessie and a bunch of her adoring fans hanging round the water fountain.

Laney was annoyed when her stomach lurched. She wasn't going to let Jessie stop her doing what she wanted.

"Better be quick. I think the bell's about to go." Steph hung back by the doors.

Laney's wet clothes stuck to her skin as she weaved her way through the group of girls and stopped in front of the fountain. She took the lid off the bottle and then dropped it. Cheeks flushing, she hurried to pick it up. Shaking the last drips out of the bottle, she pushed down the tap to turn on the fountain.

"How come you're thirsty, Laney?" said Jessie. "Is it hard work coming last round the track all the time? Don't worry, you can't help being a freak of nature."

Laney gritted her teeth as she watched the water trickle into the bottom of the bottle. She wasn't going to let Jessie have the last word. "If I'm a freak then so are you!" It wasn't a very good insult, but she couldn't think of anything better.

As she glared at Jessie, the bottle leaped in her hand and the water inside started to bubble.

"Watch it!" cried Jessie. The sneering look slipped from her face and her dark eyes widened. "What are you doing? Give me that! Get away from the fountain!" Her voice held a surprising note of panic. She tried to grab the water bottle but Laney held on to it tightly.

The bottle filled to the top and hot water splashed over their hands. The liquid inside was boiling and there was a strange, bulbous cloud of steam rising above it. The water looked beautiful, spilling out and swirling round the fountain plughole. It reminded Laney of something that she couldn't quite grasp. A memory, maybe. A forgotten moment in time.

Jessie backed away, her eyes narrowing. "What have you *done*?"

"Why's the water hot?" said Laney. "It shouldn't be hot." She reached forwards, dreamlike. As her fingers touched the fountain tap she felt a sudden jolt, like electricity, run up her arm.

A deep boom echoed along the corridor and time seemed to slow down as the tap exploded and the fountain split right off the wall. Water gushed from the exposed pipes in the wall and ceiling, flooding the passage in a matter of seconds.

Laney slipped, landing in the flood. Girls screamed, trying to shield themselves from the jets of spraying water. Jessie elbowed past them to be the first to the door.

Strangely calm, Laney watched them all struggling to get away. Classroom doors were flung open and people ran. The sharp voice of a teacher cut through all the shouting.

Laney got up, the water swirling round her knees. She must look so stupid – her clothes were properly soaked this time and she could feel her hair sticking to her forehead. She waded over to the door just as the metal water fountain was swept away down the corridor.

Blinding sunshine greeted her as she pushed her way through the exit, followed by a round of applause from all the kids gathered outside. Laney flushed again, feeling everyone staring at her.

"Right everybody, down to the field!" Miss Roderick rushed through the crowd in her red tracksuit. "Go to the place we use for fire drills."

"Why, Miss?" said Claudia. "It's not a fire, is it?"

"Just go where you're told, Claudia." Miss Roderick glared at her. "Hurry up, all of you! Away from the building." She hurried back and forth, rounding everyone up like a sheepdog.

Claudia stopped in front of Laney and fixed her with cat-like eyes. "What did you do in there?" she asked.

"What? Nothing!" Laney flushed. "The fountain broke."

Claudia stared unblinking for a few seconds. Then she turned in one smooth movement and joined the crowd heading for the field.

"The teachers won't blame you, will they?" said Steph nervously. "They might think it was an end-of-term joke."

Water suddenly broke through the doors and

gushed down the path, so the girls hurried away.

"I didn't do anything." Laney's voice shook. "How would I have got the fountain off the wall? There must've been a problem with the pipe or the water pressure or something."

"Well, you should know, as your dad does that sort of thing."

Laney thought for a moment. Her dad was a plumber, fixing pipes and mending leaks. She was sure he'd be able to explain why the pipes broke. What about the water in the bottle? It had looked just like it was boiling. And the tap on the fountain had exploded right at the moment she touched it.

But no one could boil water with their bare hands or make a tap explode just by touching it, could they?

A few hours later, with the water drained and the bottom corridor blocked off, the kids were allowed back in the building to fetch their things to go home. Laney kept her head down. If one more person thanked her for making them miss lessons, she thought she'd scream.

Miss Roderick caught up with her just outside the door. "Wait a minute, please, Laney. I've been told you were standing next to the fountain when it broke. Is there anything you can tell me about how it happened?" Her eyes searched Laney's face.

9

"It just came off the wall." Laney stared at the ground. She knew she should look at the teacher. She would only look guilty if she avoided her gaze. She had to remember she hadn't done anything wrong.

Well…not on purpose…

She remembered how the water fountain had felt hot under her fingers before the whole thing burst. A sick feeling grew in her stomach and rose into her chest. "Maybe the pipes behind the wall were already broken," she said, trying to steady her voice.

"I hope you're being honest about this, young lady," said Miss Roderick. "Another pupil saw you and thinks you had something to do with it. If I do find out it was you I'll be ringing your parents." She waved a hand for Laney to go.

Laney joined the tide of kids sweeping through the building. Everyone else seemed to be caught up in the end-of-term buzz, laughing and yelling as they swept down the corridor.

"Laney!" Steph had waited for her. "Are you OK? What did Roderick say?"

Laney pulled a face. "She just gave me a warning."

"But you didn't actually do anything…"

Laney could hear the doubt in Steph's voice. "I was nearest to the fountain when it broke. And it sounds like Jessie told them it was me."

The crowd was thinning now and the school

buses were starting their engines.

"You'd better go. You'll miss your bus," said Steph. "Happy birthday, anyway!"

"Thanks. I'll ring you when you're back from holiday." Laney hurried on to the bus to find that it was nearly full. She sat down on a seat as far away from Jessie as possible and took a quick look round.

The bus was divided into the usual groups. A crowd of older kids sat at the back. Laney saw Fletcher Thornbeam look at her and mutter something to his friend.

Craig Mottle, who fancied himself as the class clown, yelled, "Hey, Rivers! You've got the right name for someone who causes a flood. Rivers? Flood? Geddit?"

Laney flushed but before she could reply, Claudia interrupted. "What would be a good name for you then, Craig?" she said smoothly. "Let's ask the whole bus, shall we?"

Craig got the hint and went back to his friends. Laney smiled gratefully at Claudia, but the other girl just stared back for a moment before turning, with cat-like grace, to look out of the window.

The bus lurched away down the road, and the rows of houses and shops turned into open fields. Laney stared at the countryside without seeing it. She tried to go over everything that had happened. The taste of the water in her drinking bottle, the fountain breaking, Miss Roderick's warning...

She sank back in her seat. This was a rubbish birthday. Her reflection glared back from the window. If Miss Roderick *did* call her dad and Kim, then they might ground her for a very long time. She couldn't get stuck in Skellmore for the whole summer. Nothing ever happened in Skellmore.

Endless fields rolled past, mostly filled with sheep. The sun poured through the smeary windows, making the bus baking hot. Laney wished she had her water bottle, but she'd lost it somewhere in the chaos of the broken pipes and running kids.

The country lane widened as they rounded the corner into Skellmore High Street with its three shops and two park benches. At four o'clock on a Friday, the village was already quite empty and the air was thick with July heat.

The bus stopped and Laney stood up to get off.

"Laney?" Claudia held out a school blazer. "Is this yours?"

Laney recognised it. "Yeah, thanks." Their eyes met for a moment. Laney thought she saw a flash of something in Claudia's face. It could have been pity or annoyance, but it was gone so fast she couldn't be sure.

"Get a move on, Claudia." Fletcher Thornbeam stood behind them, his broad frame filling the aisle. "I think the driver wants to go."

"I'll move when I'm ready." Claudia handed Laney the blazer, her eyes unblinking.

"Yeah, but you know the rules," Fletcher told her, glancing pointedly at Laney. "This isn't the time or the place for a *chat*."

Claudia sighed and muttered something about rules being made to be broken.

The driver called down the bus to them, so Laney picked up her bag and hurried to the steps. Why didn't Fletcher want Claudia to talk to her? Maybe it was because of what happened today. But why would he care? Fletcher was in the year above. He didn't hang around with them at school and she barely saw him in Skellmore.

She stepped off the bus and stopped to put her blazer in her bag. Craig climbed down behind her and bashed into her arm as he went past. Claudia glided smoothly down the bus steps and walked away up the hill. Fletcher headed in the opposite direction, towards his end of the village. Jessie got off last, still shooting dagger looks at Laney.

The bus engine roared and drove away towards the next stop in Gillforth village. The other kids hurried off, leaving Laney alone on the High Street.

The wind picked up the dust on the road and sent it dancing in little swirls. The dried-up red flowers growing in the plant tub outside the corner shop looked like they hadn't seen water for weeks. An

empty crisp packet skittered across the pavement.
The place looks parched, Laney thought. She longed
for rain.

Dark clouds thickened in the sky and lightning
flashed, making her jump. A few seconds later,
thunder boomed overhead and rain began to
beat down. Laney's hair stuck to her head and
water dripped down her face, but she felt happier
somehow.

She swung her bag on to her shoulder and walked
into the storm.

CHAPTER
2

Laney walked down the High Street, past the mini-mart and the Lionhart Pet Shop. She crossed the road and took her normal shortcut through the churchyard. The church spire stretched up high, sticking right into the rainclouds as if trying to make them burst. Thunder rolled over her head again. Slowly this time, like a giant's yawn.

Laney opened the iron gate and closed it behind her. The sky grew lighter and the rain thinned, leaving water sparkling on the tilted gravestones. Wiping her wet face on her sleeve, she followed the gravel path round the side of the church and past the fenced-off pond in the corner. The clouds shifted apart, revealing blue sky and a moon that had risen early.

Laney stopped and her throat tightened. The moon was full and red, and it hung there looking down like a blood-stained face. She stared at it, wondering why it was that creepy colour. Was it a trick of the light – maybe something to do with the storm? Eventually she managed to pull her gaze away and carried on through the gate that led into her road, Oldwing Rise. Her house sat there, snug in the middle of the row of cottages.

Light poured over her as she opened the front door and the TV rumbled in the background. Her stepbrother, Toby, sat in his high chair in the kitchen, watching his favourite train programme.

"Laney! Choo-choo!" Toby rolled his little train across the kitchen table to her.

"Hi, Toby!" Laney caught the engine and rolled it back to him.

"Laney!" Her stepmum, Kim, hugged her. "Happy birthday!"

"Thanks!" Laney relaxed a little. Miss Roderick hadn't rung. Kim would have said something straight away if she had.

"Come and see what Toby and I made for you." Kim drew Laney over to a chair and placed a large, lopsided sponge cake on the table in front of her.

Laney stared at the chocolate icing and her name spelled out in Smarties. She swallowed, her heart suddenly full. "Thanks. It looks great!"

"Me want cake!" said Toby.

"Let's have it now." Laney grinned. Either they had run out of sweets on the final letter or Toby had eaten some of the Smarties off the top of the cake already.

"Are you sure you don't want to wait? I asked your dad to come home early especially," said Kim.

"He won't remember." It was a family joke that her dad never seemed to remember Laney's birthday, although today she didn't find it so funny. He had left for work early that morning before she was up, without even leaving a card.

"Let's have some candles on it, too," Laney said

daringly. She knew she was on dangerous ground.

Kim paused and looked at her. "You know we don't have any," she said evenly. "Your dad won't have anything like that in the house."

"Oh, please, Kim! Won't next-door have some?" Laney tilted her head to one side and widened her blue eyes in the look she knew Kim could never resist. "I am twelve now."

Kim made a face. "All right then. I guess you're old enough to be sensible and we can keep Toby away from them easily enough. I'll see if Mr Platt has any." She hurried away to knock on their neighbour's door.

"Cake! Cake!" Toby said, bouncing in his high chair.

"In a minute," Laney promised.

Kim returned quickly, holding a handful of candles in one hand and a box of matches in the other. "These will look lovely." She placed twelve golden candles on top of the cake. Then she struck a match and lit each one in turn. A smoky fragrance filled the room.

Laney watched, mesmerised by the little flames that danced in the draught from the back door. There was something special about them. It had been so long since she'd seen any kind of flame that she'd forgotten how pretty they were. Her dad never let them have anything in the house that burned, not even birthday candles. When she was little she used to see them on her friends' cakes every year, until they'd all got too old to have that kind of birthday party any more.

"OK, ready?" Kim smiled. She lit the final candle and blew out the match. "Toby's been practising the song, haven't you?"

"Happy bird-day to you!" sang Toby.

"*Birth*-day," corrected Kim, but Toby wasn't listening.

The front door slammed.

Kim and Laney exchanged looks. Toby went on singing.

"Should we take the candles off?" said Laney.

Kim hesitated. But it was too late.

Mr Rivers stopped in the doorway, his face darkening. "What are you doing? Put those out!"

"No, Robert. It's her birthday. Let her have the candles for once," said Kim.

"Birthday?" Her dad's eyes flicked to Laney's face. "Oh…yes, of course it is. But we're not having candles. I don't want any fire in this house." He stepped towards the cake.

Defiantly, Laney leaned over and blew the candles out. Eleven flames flickered and vanished, and eleven tiny lines of smoke curled upwards. But the twelfth candle toppled over on to the chocolate icing, its flame still burning brightly.

Toby clapped his hands. "Happy bird-day!"

"No fire in this house," repeated Mr Rivers, and he went to hang up his coat, frowning.

"They're just candles," Laney muttered after he'd gone.

"Never mind. We've still got the cake and I'll cut it up in a minute, OK?" Kim's face had a closed look as she lifted Toby out of his high chair and took him upstairs.

Laney stared down at the cake. Some birthday this was.

She reached for the fallen candle that lay on the icing with its flame still flickering. Her dad hadn't noticed it, hidden behind all the blown-out ones. Why was he so freaked out by a tiny little flame anyway? It was only a birthday candle.

She picked it up by the base and looked at the flame, noticing the blue-tinged space at the bottom and how it soared up to a pure gold point. It was just a little candle, not dangerous at all. Yet her dad would be so mad if he saw her holding it like this. What *was* the big fuss?

The candle wobbled and slipped in her grasp.

For a long moment, the flame touched the tip of her middle finger. A scorching pain spread through her skin. She grimaced and dropped the candle. The flame went out. Cross with herself, she picked it up and put it with the others. Then she rinsed her finger under cold water to soothe the stinging. So that was what it felt like to be burned. She was glad her dad hadn't seen her.

It was growing darker outside so she switched on the kitchen light. Her burned finger began to throb. There was a round mark where the flame had touched her. The soreness turned into a strange tingling that spread through her hand and up her arm. She waggled the injured finger. *As long as it hasn't dropped off you'll be fine*, her dad used to say when she was little. Well, it hadn't dropped off but she didn't feel fine.

She could hear voices in the living room arguing in low whispers.

"Why shouldn't she have birthday candles for once?" Kim was saying. "What's wrong with that?"

Mr Rivers' gruff reply was too faint to be heard.

Guilt twisted in Laney's stomach. She was the one who'd made Kim fetch the candles. She hadn't meant to cause trouble between them. Quickly she gathered up the blown-out candles and the matches and threw them in the bin.

The pain in her hand and arm grew stronger, spreading relentlessly into the rest of her body. It began as a horrible sort of prickliness that made her want to scratch like mad and then turned into an overpowering agony. She doubled over on the kitchen floor, grasping at the tiles with her fingertips.

She tried to call Kim but no sound came out. Her heart hammered. She felt as if every tiny bit of her was changing from the inside – every cell inside her was shifting. Then, just as she thought she couldn't bear it any more, the pain vanished.

Hauling herself up, she leaned on the kitchen worktop, relieved to be free of the pain. Her reflection in the kitchen window looked strange. Her skin was pale and her eyes gleamed, almost as though there was a ring of bright gold encircling each pupil. The burn mark on her finger glowed red.

Cross voices rose in the living room and a door opened. She panicked. She didn't want them to see her like this. Taking one last look at her strange eyes, she ducked through the back door and closed it behind her. Then she rushed down the passage that ran alongside the house and across the road to the churchyard. From there she crossed the High Street and took the footpath that led out of Skellmore towards the riverbank. The Mistray river was the best thing about living in Skellmore and she often came down here to think. The sun vanished below the horizon and the light faded.

The pain didn't return. It was replaced by a feeling of warmth, as if melted chocolate was flowing through her bloodstream. She ran past the last row of houses and sprang down the grassy slope to the edge of the river. It was darker now and the trees on the other side of the water were no more than black shapes against a fading sky.

Now that she was away from the houses, she could see the blood-red moon again. Her heart tightened as she realised how grisly it looked, here in the gathering dark. The crimson circle matched the shape and colour of the burn on her middle finger.

She shivered. This moon was bad news. She didn't know why, but it made her feel hollow inside. A red moon – it was hard to stop looking at it.

She pulled her eyes away and looked down at the glittering river. The water stilled and her reflection became clearer in the red moonlight. For a moment she couldn't breathe. There she was, her face as pale as usual, with wisps of hair hanging over her forehead. But now there were bright golden rings in her eyes.

CHAPTER 3

Laney wasn't sure how long she'd stood there on the riverbank, staring at herself in the water. Her eyes had always been blue like her dad's, but now there were gold rings around her pupils. She hadn't really believed it when she'd seen her reflection in the kitchen window. Out here they seemed to glow even brighter.

She stumbled back up the bank, aware of the red moon watching her from above the trees. She could hear voices. There were people coming down the path from the direction of the village.

Heart thumping, she left the path and crossed the field towards the line of fences that marked the back gardens on the edge of Skellmore. She didn't want to meet anyone; didn't want them to see her like this. Reaching the first fence, she followed it, running her hand along the rough panel.

A bitter smell hung in the air, which became stronger the further she walked. She covered her nose with her hand. If she followed these fences she should come to a corner and be able to get back to the High Street and then home. She heard voices again and hurried on.

She was close to the edge of the field and she could just make out a cluster of willow and birch trees beyond. The light from the red moon strengthened, casting a revolting rusty glow across the ground. A bank of fog was rising in front of the trees. A warning pinged in Laney's mind. She'd seen fog around here lots of times, but it rose from the river, not from the woods.

Inching closer to the trees, Laney tried to remember what this place looked like in daylight. It was a pretty spot, with a good view of the river. Kim had brought her and Toby for a picnic here once. They had sat in the shade of the trees and Kim had pointed out a circle of darker grass that she called a fairy ring.

The fog near the trees rose higher. It had reached about head height and it looked orangey-red in the light from the moon. A strange heaviness weighed on Laney's chest and she struggled to breathe. It was nice here in the daytime, but this was surely some nightmare version of the place. She didn't like it. It was time to go.

She climbed over the stile and tried to find the footpath. Panic shot through her. She didn't want the fog to touch her. It looked so wrong. The way it was swaying and curling made it seem alive.

Seeing the path beneath her feet, she remembered – this was where the fairy ring had been, just here on the left. She glanced that way and froze.

Through the reddish fog she could see a black shape. It was large but close to the ground, and as she stared she realised that it was a crouching figure. An overwhelming sense of darkness and fear flooded through her.

The figure wasn't moving.

She watched it for a minute and the freezing fog folded itself around her, chilling her skin and clouding her eyes. Taking a deep breath, she tried to calm her heartbeat but the fog tasted bitter and the panic wouldn't let her go. The bitter taste filled her lungs and cold began to steal through her body as if she was being frozen from the inside.

Backing away, she hoped desperately that the figure wouldn't see her. As she breathed in more of the fog, the iciness inside her grew. She pressed a hand to her chest, but couldn't feel her body beneath the cold. Each step backwards became more difficult as the frozen feeling spread along her arms and legs.

Then the figure turned its head. It rose upwards, doubling in height, tall and faceless in the fog. Laney stared, shivering. From behind the figure came a faint, wordless singing.

The fog thickened, enclosing her in its orange-red arms and drawing her in. It brought the singing closer. She couldn't understand any of the words, but the singing told her that everything would be all right. It would all be over soon. She found herself wanting to move closer and hear more of the song.

Her foot hit an uneven piece of ground and she fell over. She put her arms out and landed on her hands and knees. She told herself to get up. She knew the dark figure was still close. More than anything else, she knew she had to run.

Laney struggled up and limped away until she splashed into shallow water and realised she'd run straight into the river. Water swirled round her ankles, soaking into her socks and shoes. A crimson colour seeped outwards from where she was standing, and the icy feeling inside went with it, until she felt like she could move properly again. The weird colour spread across the water like ink, but there was no time to think about what it meant.

Spinning round, she jumped back on to the bank and ran alongside the river until she reached the footpath. She wanted to look behind her to see if the figure was following, but she didn't dare. When she got to the first house on the street she finally turned around. There was no black figure and no fog. She was safe.

She kept on running. Skellmore seemed quiet and normal. The streetlights were bright and the houses were lit behind their curtains. It was just another summer's evening, except for that creepy red moon. She scanned the sky, but a bank of cloud had moved in and the moon had disappeared.

She hurried back home and let herself in the back door. There was no one in the kitchen but some dinner had been left out for her on the side. The birthday cake sat on the table, cut into slices but still uneaten.

"Laney? Are you OK?" called Kim from the living room. "Let me come and heat your dinner up for you."

"No, don't worry. I've got a headache so I'm not that hungry," Laney called back. She grabbed a slice of cake and went upstairs before Kim could come out to check on her.

She switched on the light in her room and looked at the finger she'd hurt on the candle flame. The red burn mark was still as bright as before.

Now for the thing she really had to know…

She took a deep breath and turned towards the mirror. Scraping her hair back from her face, she made herself walk right up to the glass. A pair of gold-ringed eyes blinked back at her. So it was true. Her eyes were different now. *She* was different.

She closed her eyes and opened them wide again. The gold circles were still there, like rings around her pupils. It reminded her of a picture of an eagle she'd once seen.

She sat down heavily on her bed, ignoring her sore finger. When she was very young and before her dad had married Kim, they'd been walking in the woods together. She had thought she'd seen a person flying, but her dad had told her it was an owl. She'd always remembered how it had swooped away, with its wingtips brushing against the leaves.

And there was an old story about an Eagle Man who had lived near Skellmore and had flown over the woods at night. They'd learned the story at primary school – how the Eagle Man had turned the whole village into eagles and then they couldn't change back into people again.

Was that what she was now – an Eagle Girl? Had the dark figure by the trees turned her into something that wasn't human? She shivered. She couldn't go back there to find out. There had been something so terrible about that figure.

Anyway, her eyes had turned gold *before* she saw the figure. She'd seen them in her reflection in the kitchen window. So maybe it was nothing to do with the dark figure at all. Maybe some people's eyes changed colour as they grew up. She'd heard somewhere that babies' eyes could change colour.

She closed her eyes and tried to breathe slowly. Her mind went back to the river. It had always been her favourite place – she loved the sound of the water.

A gentle brush of air touched her face. She opened her eyes and stood up, searching for what had made the draught. The school clothes she had been wearing were gone, and in their place was a pale-blue dress. Two translucent shapes curved out from her back, flexing as she put her hand over her mouth. They glinted, reflecting the light of the ceiling lamp.

How could they be real?

These shining wings.

CHAPTER 4

Laney stared into the mirror for a long time. Wings? That was impossible!

And she realised that she wasn't standing any more; she was hovering just above the carpet. Her start of surprise launched her upwards, and she bumped her head on the ceiling. Trying not to laugh, she flew back down and landed clumsily on the bed. Flying was obviously harder than it looked.

She stood in front of the mirror again, this time willing her feet to stay on the floor. Even her skin looked different – almost glowing. But it was the wings that she couldn't stop gazing at. They reached far above her head and curved down in a graceful arc to meet her back. She reached round to touch them. They were silky smooth. These weren't eagle wings. Eagle wings were feathery. These weren't like bird's wings at all. She wasn't sure exactly what they were, except that they were like the shape of a butterfly.

Her heart raced. Almost as if they were connected to her rising excitement, the wings began to beat and she found herself lifting off the ground again. She darted a look at her bedroom window, which was open just a little. Did she dare go out? After all, wings were for flying and she couldn't do that properly in here.

She heard a snuffling cry from Toby's room next door. He was probably making noises in his sleep again. There were footsteps on the stairs and a door opened. It would be Kim going in to check on Toby.

Laney panicked. She didn't want Kim to find her like this. She switched off the light and climbed under her duvet. She could pretend she was asleep if anyone came in.

She heard Toby's door close and the footsteps paused outside her room. Then they went away, back down the stairs.

Laney let out a long breath and sat up in bed. In her haste, she hadn't closed the curtains. The clouds had cleared, revealing the red full moon, now risen even higher in the sky. It cast an eerie glow over the houses and trees.

Laney thought she saw figures moving near the end of the lane, but when she opened the window wider and leaned out to look she couldn't see anyone. She put a hand over her shoulder to touch her wings again, but they'd disappeared and she was back in her school clothes. Exhausted, she took them off and pulled on pyjamas before falling asleep. Dreams came to her, of rippling red water and a figure wearing a long black hood.

Laney woke up with a sense of purpose the next morning. Yesterday had been scary, but now she knew a bit more. She'd had some kind of transformation and now she had wings! At least, she'd had wings for a few minutes last night.

She checked her back. Nothing. She tried closing her eyes and wishing for them to appear, but they didn't.

Clearly her wings were a little random.

She stared at her gold-ringed eyes in the mirror. Maybe her new eyes and the wings were all connected with the disaster at the water fountain yesterday. She was sure she'd made that happen somehow. She just didn't know exactly how.

Maybe she had some kind of powers and she should start by working out exactly what they were. She would begin by going back to the river. When she'd stumbled into it last night she had felt different – stronger somehow. She needed to work out why.

But if that dark figure was there… Laney shivered. She didn't want to see *that* again, but maybe it had just been a joke – someone playing a trick in the dark. She hesitated. She had to go and find out more, and it was daylight now so there was nothing to be scared of.

Slipping out of the back door, she made her way down Oldwing Rise and cut through a field at the bottom of the lane. She wasn't likely to meet anyone this way and she didn't want people to see her gold-ringed eyes.

The footpath to the river felt different in daytime – safe and familiar. She'd come down here a hundred times. She skirted along the back by the fences and approached the cluster of trees where she'd seen the fog the night before.

A figure crouched on the riverbank nearby. Laney stopped, panic tightening her chest.

The figure stood up and flicked long dark hair over her shoulders. She was staring intently into the river.

Laney's heart rate slowed again. What was Claudia doing here? She couldn't have been the person who was standing in the fog last night. She wasn't tall enough.

Claudia swung round as if she could hear Laney's thoughts. Wanting to hide her eyes, Laney pulled her sunglasses out of her jeans pocket and put them on before she walked down the slope towards the river.

"Laney. What are you doing here?" said Claudia.

Laney was surprised at the grim note in her voice. Claudia usually sounded so cool. "I just came for a walk."

"Really? Is that the only reason you're here?" Claudia turned back to the water.

Laney ducked past a hawthorn bush and hurried down the slope. Once she got closer she could see what Claudia was staring at. A large patch of river water was bright red. The colour stretched across to the opposite bank and several metres downstream.

Laney swallowed. With all the other things that had happened last night, she'd forgotten that she'd stumbled into the river and seen a weird colour spread into the water. But why wasn't it washing away?

She pushed back her hair. "I wonder what happened to the river – it looks weird." She tried to sound like she didn't care.

Claudia swung round and frowned. Her eyes had bright golden rings circling the black pupils.

"Your eyes are the same!" gasped Laney. "They're gold like mine."

"What? Show me your eyes!" said Claudia.

Laney slowly took off her sunglasses.

"You've changed," said Claudia. "Wow! I didn't think that was possible. I thought you were stuck halfway somehow. These last few weeks I couldn't work out if you even knew that you were making things happen. Then you busted the water fountain yesterday and I bet you did this too." She jerked her head at the stained river.

Laney opened her mouth to speak but didn't know what to say, so she just nodded.

"Did you change last night?" Claudia carried on. "You must have done. You weren't Awake when I saw you on the bus yesterday."

"What do you mean, awake?" Laney struggled for words. "I don't get it. I know I must have powers

– all the things that happened yesterday…"

"You've put us in serious danger of being discovered. Talk about drawing attention to yourself! Why can't you be more careful? Just look at this water."

"I'm not *trying* to do anything!" Laney was stung by her words. "Tell me what's going on."

"Haven't you guessed it yet?" Claudia's eyes widened. "Seriously?"

Laney swallowed again. "If you know what's happening to me – just tell me, please!"

"I'm surprised you haven't worked it out." Claudia looked at her pityingly. "You're a faerie."

"What? A *faerie*!" The world seemed to tilt sideways for a moment. "Are you joking?"

Claudia gave a half-smile. "I'm totally serious. You've just Awoken into your full powers. That's why your eyes have turned gold. You're a faerie. Just like me."

The air around her trembled for a moment and then a dark girl with an amber dress stood in her place. It was Claudia. Except it wasn't quite Claudia. Her skirt shimmered at the edges and behind her curved a pair of long, pale wings. Her skin looked luminous, as if it was lit from inside.

"Wow!" said Laney. "That's so… Can you make yourself change like that just by deciding to?"

"Yes. We have a human form and a faerie form.

See?" The air shimmered around her and suddenly there was the everyday Claudia.

"I had wings last night, but then they vanished," said Laney.

"You'll get used to changing into faerie form when you want to. It just takes a little practice."

"But aren't faeries...smaller?"

"No, we're not," snapped Claudia. "And even if no one else told you, you must have realised that something was going on around here. Some days I'm surprised all the humans don't notice. Of course, if you turn the river red, that doesn't *exactly* help." She turned back to look at the weird stretch of crimson water. "The cats told me about it and I thought straight away it might be you."

"The cats told you?"

Claudia nodded. "Dizzy tells me everything."

This was another confusing thought to add to the swarm in Laney's head. Claudia talked to cats and they were both faeries...

The relief was huge – she wasn't the only one who was different. But at the same time, she'd imagined having powers that no one else had and that had been pretty exciting.

And who else was in on this secret? A picture of Jessie Weir's face popped into her head. No. She couldn't be. Surely a faerie would be nicer.

"Are there other people who are faeries in

Skellmore?" she asked Claudia. "And how did I change into one anyway? And—"

"You really didn't notice anything all these years, did you?" said Claudia, half amused and half exasperated. "We'd better—" She broke off as a loud mew interrupted her. A black cat wound itself round her ankles. "All right! Calm down, Dizzy!"

The cat carried on mewing then it ran off into the undergrowth.

"Dizzy says there's trouble on the way," said Claudia. "The tribes are anxious. Cats know these things because they're very sensitive. Also they love listening in on everyone else's conversations."

Laney opened her mouth and closed it again. Tribes? What tribes?

"You need to talk to an Elder. I'd better take you to see Gwen," said Claudia. "She's probably the best person to tell you everything."

"Who's Gwen?"

"You know, Mrs Whitefern."

"Oh." Laney knew Mrs Whitefern well. Or she thought she did. She'd been living in Skellmore for years and always let children come and have milk and cookies in her sitting room. Mrs Whitefern was just about the most ordinary little old lady Laney could think of, apart from all the funny hats she had. It was a Skellmore joke that Mrs Whitefern owned more hats than the rest of the village put together.

"What did you do to your hand?" said Claudia.

Laney looked at her finger. The red mark had faded but was still clearly visible. "I burned it yesterday on a candle."

"You're a right disaster area," said Claudia. "Let's go before you do any more damage. Gwen will know what should be done about the river."

Laney took another look at the water and then followed Claudia up the slope. They drew nearer to the clump of trees where she'd seen the crouching shadow the night before. She pictured the shape of the figure as it had turned its face towards her, and shivered. At once she began to hear the faint sound of singing, but this time it wasn't a comforting sound. It sounded bleak and cold, and made her think of stars and comets and endless black Space.

"Can you hear that singing?" Laney walked towards the sound, not really knowing what her feet were doing.

Claudia grabbed her arm and pulled her backwards. "Don't go over there!" she said crossly. "You're getting too close to the faerie ring. Don't go near them, OK? They're dangerous." She let go of Laney and turned away.

Laney stared at the faerie ring. The dark circle of grass looked normal enough and she couldn't hear the singing any more. Curious, she took a step towards the ring. Instantly the voices resumed their high, piercing song that made goose bumps rise on her arms.

To one side of the ring, on a section of flattened grass, lay a tiny mound of greyish dust. As the voices sang, a pinch of the dust floated into the air and swirled round until it was sucked down into the centre of the faerie ring and vanished completely.

Laney backed away. She must have walked over that circle of grass millions of times before and hardly even noticed it was there. Claudia said that the ring was dangerous; weird then that it should seem so enchanting at the same time.

CHAPTER
5

Laney followed Claudia, but hung back when they reached the first houses in the village. "I don't want everyone to see my eyes," she said, putting her sunglasses back on.

"Humans can't see the change. Only other faeries can see it. Remember, you never saw the gold in my eyes before you Awoke," said Claudia.

"I guess so." Laney glanced around. She was still expecting someone to jump out and yell, "*Fooled you!*" But nobody did.

"Are you ready?" A mischievous smile curved on Claudia's face.

"Sure." Laney felt pretty nervous, but there was no way she was going to admit it.

They passed a row of houses, followed a bend in the road and Skellmore High Street came into view. The pavement seemed washed clean by yesterday's storm, and the dust and dirt had gone.

Laney had always thought it was silly calling the place a High Street when it was only two shops and a hairdresser's opposite a park. Hardly anyone shopped there because there was so little to buy. But today the place looked quite busy. There were two cars parked by the minimart and a group of people standing outside the Lionhart Pet Shop.

Laney lifted up her sunglasses to look more carefully. Something else was different too. What was it?

A swarm of white petals came swooping down the road. She ducked instinctively and then watched them fly away behind her. She thought she heard a tiny laugh.

"Did you see that? What was—" Laney turned and saw another cloud of white things zooming round the big oak tree in the park. "Look! There's more!" She pointed at the oak tree and froze.

A wave of light rolled up the tree trunk from the ground. It turned branch after branch and leaf after leaf to gold, until the whole tree gleamed for an instant. The branches reached higher into the sky, as if the tree was stretching. The next moment the flush of gold vanished and the branches and leaves returned to normal.

Claudia grinned. "Now that you have faerie eyes, things might look a tiny bit different."

Laney took a few steps forwards. The branches of the oak tree waved like there was an invisible breeze and the ground in the park seemed to ripple. On the corner by the churchyard gate, a bunch of cats clustered together as if they were having a conversation. They stopped all at once to look at Laney. There was a buzzing in the air and it made Laney's skin tingle.

"What's happening?" she breathed.

"Nothing new. It's like this every day. You've just never been able to see it before," said Claudia. "It's because there's a faerie ring here in the village in the middle of the park and power seeps out of it. Not many places are as faerie-like as Skellmore."

"Why did the oak tree turn gold?"

"It's so close to the faerie ring that it sucks up a lot of power."

"It's so weird that most people can't see it happening."

Claudia shrugged. "That's just the way it works, I guess."

"What are those white things in the air?"

"They're sprites – they're OK."

Laney's eyes grew rounder as she followed Claudia down the High Street. The puddles on the pavement seemed to shimmer as she passed. She stopped to gaze into one and in the watery reflection she saw the air glittering around her.

"Keep going." Claudia tugged her arm. "You're making it too obvious."

But Laney hardly noticed what Claudia was saying. She goggled at the house on the corner of Gnarlwood Lane where Mr and Mrs Willowby lived. She passed the house every day on the bus to school. She'd never really looked closely at it before, but she was sure it had been made of bricks just the same as any other building. Not any more.

The outside of the house looked like a rough tree trunk and several leafy struts joined together to form a tree-like roof.

"Laney!" hissed Claudia.

Laney jumped, realising she'd stepped into the road in her eagerness to look closer.

"I'll show you round the place afterwards, OK?" muttered Claudia. "Let's just get to Gwen's house first."

They passed several people with normal faces. Then Claudia's brother, Tom, sauntered past and Laney drew in her breath sharply as she saw the gold rings in his eyes. She was glad she was wearing her sunglasses so that he couldn't see hers.

"Mum wants you in the shop, little sis," he told Claudia.

"OK, I'm going." Claudia let him pass and then whispered to Laney. "Go to Gwen's. You know where she lives, don't you? I'll catch you up in a bit."

Laney nodded and the two girls separated.

Laney sped up. There was something strange about the group of adults standing outside the pet shop. Fletcher's parents, the Thornbeams, were among them. The group fell silent as she passed. Someone opened the shop door. Underneath the sound of kittens mewing and guinea pigs squeaking, the buzzing in the air became stronger.

She darted a look at the pet shop and nearly fell over. She was expecting a red-brick building with rainbow letters over the door that spelled "Lionhart

Pet Shop". But instead there was a furry-looking dark-brown wall. The shop name was the same, but set into the wall just above it was a gigantic pair of cat's eyes staring out at everyone. As Laney looked, the vivid-green eyes turned in her direction. A huge mouth filled with sharp teeth opened in the wall and hissed.

Stumbling over her feet, Laney fixed her eyes on the pavement and hurried on. The adults resumed their conversation and she caught a sentence as she went by.

"The red moon – this is the first one for years – it could be a catastrophe…"

Laney's heart pounded. They were talking about the red moon from last night. The mention of it reminded her how scared she'd been and she was relieved when she reached the end of the High Street.

She crossed the road and turned into Gnarlwood Lane. Now that she was closer, she couldn't help staring at the tree-like house all over again. The walls seemed exactly like a rough tree trunk, and she longed to go right up and touch them. Mr Willowby was out in his front garden, sweeping the path.

Laney carried on to the house next door, which looked even stranger. This was Mrs Whitefern's house and she knew it very well, having been inside so many times when she was younger. But she had never seen it like this. The walls were completely covered by ivy, and the roof was made from five gigantic trumpet-shaped white flowers all clustered together. As she gazed, one of the trumpet flowers swayed and a cloud of green smoke drifted out and got carried away by the breeze.

Laney took off her sunglasses to get a better look before walking over to the gate at the bottom of the front path. There was a noise behind her and Sara Thornbeam, Fletcher's little sister, stood there with a group of her friends. Laney wondered how they'd sneaked up on her so easily.

"You've changed," said Sara. "I thought you were human."

Laney's cheeks flushed. "Um, yeah. So did I." Sara looked so strange with gold-ringed eyes. Laney couldn't believe that she was a part of all this too.

Sara ran off calling, "Fletcher, guess what?"

The other children carried on staring at Laney.

Laney's insides felt shaky. She didn't think she could stand being stared at by anyone else right now. She hurried up the path, but before she reached the ivy-covered front door, it opened and Mrs Whitefern stood in the doorway. She wore a green dress, which wrinkled over her short, round figure. On her head was a velvety purple hat with a sprig of lavender on the brim.

"Off you go, children. Go and play," she called in her high voice.

The children scattered.

Mrs Whitefern smiled warmly. "I've been expecting you, Laney."

CHAPTER
6

Laney had expected Gwen's eyes to be golden, but they were tawny just as they'd always been. She wasn't sure they looked very different. She couldn't help gazing at them, trying to work out if there was any change.

"Hello, Mrs Whitefern," she said awkwardly. "Claudia said I should come and see you." Suddenly she wondered if this was a good idea. Mrs Whitefern couldn't be the same as her. She just couldn't be.

"Yes, come in. It's nice to have you to visit. Of course, you used to come here when you were little, but I think you really came for my cookies back then. It's lucky that I baked a fresh batch of them this morning." Gwen tottered into the front room, which was filled with the scent of cookies. The smell brought back the memory of all the times Laney had been there when she was younger.

"I think I should go," said Laney. "This must be a mistake."

"No, there's no mistake, my dear." Gwen hobbled to the sofa and plumped the cushions. "Sit down and have something to eat." She offered Laney a plate stacked high with duck-shaped cookies.

Laney edged towards the door. "I'm sorry, Mrs Whitefern. I didn't mean to… I should go."

"But you've only just got here." Gwen looked at her beadily. "Someone as old and little as me can hardly understand what you're going through, is that what you're thinking?"

"Um, it's just that I have to get back." Laney tried to smile politely. She was pretty sure that Mrs Whitefern couldn't help her, but she didn't want to be rude.

Gwen tottered over to a fruit bowl that stood on a side table. She peeled an orange and took a pip from one of the segments. Holding it in the palm of her crinkly hand, she whispered to it and then blew softly. It sprouted instantly, growing a sturdy stem, then several side branches, all with leaves. Within half a minute there were ripe oranges hanging from each branch of the tree. It carried on growing and sprouting until it reached the ceiling.

Laney stared wide-eyed at Gwen through the tangle of branches. This was the same Gwen. She just hadn't really known her before. "That was amazing! I didn't think you were…like that…" She tailed off.

"I know." Gwen picked an orange and offered it to Laney with a wrinkled smile. "Sometimes you have to see with the heart not with the eyes. Not all power lies in young skin and supple limbs."

"I'm sorry!" Laney blushed as she took the orange.

Gwen placed the orange tree, now bushy with overhanging roots, carefully on the carpet. "It seems we must start afresh. I am Gwen, faerie Elder and the oldest Thorn faerie in Skellmore."

She stood a little taller as she spoke, power shining from behind her tawny eyes.

Laney sat down heavily on the flowery sofa. She thought she knew this room. She remembered the threadbare bit on the arm of the sofa where you could see the white lining underneath. Yet all the time Gwen had kept her secret. She took hold of a rose-patterned cushion and held it tight. "So it's all true then? About the…" She couldn't bring herself to say the word faeries.

"You *are* a faerie, Laney," Gwen said solemnly. "There are faeries living in different places all over the world and this village is one of them."

Laney shook her head. "But this is just Skellmore!"

Gwen smiled and tucked her curly white hair under her hat. "There's more to this village than you think. Come with me. There's something I want to show you." She tottered through the door and down the passageway. "Usually I keep my front room as ordinary as possible. Then I use my skills down here in my plant house," she called back.

Laney skirted round the orange tree and followed her down the passage. Even though she'd been to Gwen's house millions of times, she'd never been any further than the front room before.

They passed through a doorway hung with long curling vines and the scent of flowers filled the air. Then she was inside a huge plant house with two glass walls and a glass ceiling. Small trees stretched up to the windowed panes in the roof. Flowers grew beneath them in crimson, pink and mauve.

"It's beautiful!" said Laney.

"This is the part of my house I could never let you see before you Awakened," said Gwen.

They followed the path, which was almost covered with foliage. The flowers turned their faces towards Gwen as she passed. A nearby tree branch moved creakily to rest its leaves on her shoulder. Laney caught her breath.

"Come and sit down." Gwen slowly seated herself on a wooden bench with long vines woven all around it. The flowers gazed at the old lady with upturned faces. Laney noticed that the backs of Gwen's hands were covered with curling silvery marks that she'd never seen before.

"Other Elders said that you might never Awaken," Gwen told her. "They said that twelve was too old. But there was just something about you – something waiting to come out. That's why I've been expecting you to come here."

"But why did I change… I mean, Awaken?" said Laney.

"Your faerie self was always inside you, waiting. Maybe it was simply the right time for it to come alive," said Gwen. "Awakening must happen to each faerie, otherwise their power stays locked inside them. The power of your tribe has now been set free."

Laney's mind whirled with questions. "What's a tribe? Claudia said something about that too."

"Your tribe describes the root of your power, and in time they will become like your family," said Gwen. "I am from the Thorn tribe. We draw our strength from plants and trees, and in turn we use our powers to help them."

"Am I a Thorn faerie?" said Laney.

Gwen looked at her steadily and Laney suddenly wondered how much she could see with those penetrating eyes. "No, I don't think you are," Gwen told her. "But the Thornbeam family are Thorns and so are the Willowbys."

Laney thought of Fletcher and his little sister Sara, both Thorn faeries. But what was she? "What are the other tribes called?" she asked.

"There are five tribes altogether. The Greytails have power over any creature on the land. Then the Kestrels have power over the air. The Blaze tribe can control fire and the Mist tribe have power over water." Gwen smiled. "There are no Kestrel or Blaze faeries living in Skellmore, although we sometimes see them passing through."

"Thorn, Kestrels, Blaze and Greytails?" said Laney.

"And Mist," said Gwen.

"And Mist," Laney repeated, pushing back the tendrils of hair that fell over her forehead. She felt as though the world was tilting sideways again, just like it had when Claudia had told her she was a faerie.

She had to know what tribe she belonged to. What power did she have? She sprang up from the bench and stared at her reflection in the window. The answer was staring her in the face. No wonder she'd made the water fountain explode.

"I have power over water." She turned to Gwen. "I'm a Mist faerie, aren't I?"

"Yes, I think you are," said Gwen with a smile.

The front door banged and Claudia ran down the passageway. "Did you know there's an orange tree in the middle of your sitting room?"

"Help yourself if you'd like any fruit," said Gwen. "You did the right thing by sending Laney to me."

Claudia grinned. "I don't think I was explaining things very well."

"I get it now," said Laney. "I'm a Mist faerie." It felt strange to say it.

"Well, duh!" Claudia grinned. "Don't get me wet, OK? I don't like water."

"But why is this happening in Skellmore?" said Laney. "I thought this was the most boring place on the planet."

"It *is* quite boring here," agreed Claudia. "My

mum and dad won't even let me fly on my own half the time! I had to sneak out of the window last night."

Laney blinked. She had a picture in her head of Claudia flying out of the window, her pale wings shimmering in the dark. "I'd like to learn to fly."

"You have to be careful that none of the humans see you." Claudia climbed on to a garden table and leaned back languidly. "Although people could work out what's going on if they tried a bit harder. They could totally spot the different tribes, for a start. I mean, have you ever wondered why some people can make anything grow? That's typical Thorn tribe. And people who dash about like a whirlwind – well, that's your Kestrel tribe. As for us Greytails, well, we're the best, of course…"

"Claudia, Laney needs time to take all of this in." Gwen's high voice grew stern.

Claudia carried on. "But it amazes me that humans never notice. And – oh! We haven't told you how many famous faeries there are. Queen Elizabeth the First was a Greytail, but only because her mother, Anne Boleyn, was and—"

"Claudia!" said Gwen.

Laney struggled for a moment with her whirling thoughts. "But…where do you – I mean we – come from? And why do you live as if you're the same as humans?"

"In the beginning we called ourselves the 'Fair Eyes', because only we could see the golden circles in our eyes that made us different," said Gwen solemnly. "Time went by, and the name became shorter. 'Fair Eyes' became 'faeries'. But the secret of our existence was kept hidden. Any stories about us faded into legend." She fixed Laney with her gaze. "You must give your word that you will keep this secret, always."

"Can we tell her the Tale of the First Faeries?" said Claudia.

Gwen didn't reply. She watched Laney unwaveringly.

"I won't tell anyone, I promise," said Laney, wondering who would believe her anyway.

"Be sure you keep to your promise. Bad things will happen if you choose to break it. Now..." Gwen's tone lightened and her little-old-lady manner returned. "The Tale of the First Faeries, did you say, Claudia? Let me see if I've got any Spirit Smoke in the cupboard." She got up and went down the passageway, returning a minute later with a dark-blue bottle. "I haven't done this for a while." She clicked her fingers and a long vine dropped down to hold the bottle suspended in the air.

"What does it do?" said Laney.

"It's the tale of faeries from long ago," said Claudia. "It's a great story!"

"It's not just a story," Gwen said seriously. "This is faerie lore, part of the ancient wisdom of our people." She took the stopper out of the bottle and thin grey smoke began to curl over the top. It swayed from side to side and then spread slowly outwards, turning from grey to all the colours of the rainbow.

Laney started to see shapes inside the smoke – mountains and people and trees. She wanted to reach out and touch them.

Gwen cleared her throat. "For hundreds of years, faeries lived in their tribes far away from humans. The Thorns lived deep in the forest."

At Gwen's words, Laney saw great green forests sprouting in the smoke. She could even smell the earth and leaves.

"The Greytails ran with packs of animals," continued Gwen, and Laney saw a pack of wolves running under a full moon. She could almost feel the earth beneath their feet, it seemed so real.

"The Mist tribes dwelled by the water, loving the quiet ways of the pond and stream…" As Gwen's voice tailed away, Laney saw dragonflies skimming across a river, the sapphire sheen on their wings catching the sun.

"The Blaze and Kestrel tribes had their favourite places too." At this, Laney saw the dancing flames of a fire and then a bird circling high in the air. She could feel the wind on her face.

"But as time passed, the forests were cut down and the humans hunted the animals for food. Life became hard for the faeries, so they secretly began to live among humans in order to survive. They learned to disguise themselves, joining in with human ways until they couldn't remember why they'd ever stayed apart." Laney watched the scene change as all the faeries' wings vanished and they blended in with other people. She felt a little sad.

"Although they were hidden, the faeries never forgot what they were and each tribe forged a sacred object to hold the essence of their power. These were called the Myricals and they were very precious."

The smoke changed colour and formed five objects. There was a wooden arrow, a pale wolf figurine, a slim transparent bottle, a scarred grey rock and a bright mirror. Laney leaned forwards to look at them more closely, but the images faded. Then the smoke turned grey again and curled away into nothing.

"And that's how we came to be here, living with everyone else," said Gwen. "That's our faerie history and that's how it's told to each new faerie that Awakens. Although not many get to see the story by Spirit Smoke."

"Cool, huh?" Claudia jumped down off the table

and stretched.

"But it's sad, really – the way they had to change their lives," said Laney. "How weird to have magic power but be forced to hide it…" She stopped, suddenly realising that's exactly how Gwen and Claudia were living.

"Listen to me, Laney," said Gwen. "You must not let humans know what you are. This is the most dangerous time. Your powers are completely new and you're not in control of them yet. Every thought, every feeling, could make something happen."

"She's already made something happen," said Claudia. "She changed the colour of the river, down by the bridge. I bet the other faerie Elders will go mad when they find it. They're already freaking out about some red moon."

"A red moon?" Gwen said quickly. "Claudia? Are you sure that's what they were saying?"

"Yes, they said the moon was red last night. They were really stressed about it."

"They don't know the red river was caused by me, though?" Laney bit her lip.

"It won't take them long to figure it out. One of the Thorns saw you looking at the cat eyes on our pet shop wall, so they must've known you could see them. It's a good thing you had your sunglasses on. You'll have to tell everyone you've Awakened soon, though."

Claudia stopped, turning to look at Gwen, who had risen from the bench, her face creased in thought. "A red moon – this is unexpected." The old lady walked slowly back and forth. "I was working on potions last night so I did not go out, but I knew there was something… The trees felt a change deep down in their roots."

"When my mum was talking about a red moon, she said something about a child of a *weaver*," said Claudia.

Gwen continued tottering up and down the plant house, ignoring the two girls for a moment. The curling silvery marks on her hands stood out clearly. "Is this really the moment that the prophecy speaks of?" she muttered to herself. "Is it really so soon?"

"What's wrong?" said Claudia. "I don't understand what's so bad about the moon looking like that. Is it a Thorn tribe thing?"

Gwen stopped in front of Laney and now her kindliness had vanished. "I must go and find the other Elders. Where are they, Claudia?"

There was a bang at the front door.

Claudia ran halfway down the passageway. She looked back, her face serious. "Um, you'll never believe it, but they're outside right now."

CHAPTER 7

"Take Laney and go!" Gwen commanded. "Get out the back way. If you're careful maybe even the Greytails won't hear you."

"Sure – easy!" said Claudia.

Laney jumped as she heard more hammering on the front door. "Will they be angry with me?"

"I'll tell them that you've Awakened, but I need to talk to them alone." Gwen straightened her velvet hat and headed for the passageway with surprising speed. "You can meet them properly later on. Quickly now, my dear. Follow Claudia."

Laney followed Claudia out of the side door as Gwen went to let her visitors in at the front. Claudia skulked through the jungle-like garden and climbed a tree in the corner, which had a cluster of low branches.

"You can climb, can't you?" said Claudia, springing off the branch and over the fence in a graceful bound.

Laney heard voices coming from the house and shrank back behind a screen of leaves. The fence didn't look easy to get over but if Claudia had done it then surely she could too. "Of course I can climb." She heaved herself on to the lowest branch and tried to swing one leg over the fence.

The way that Gwen had hurried her out of the door made her nervous. What were the other Elders like and who were they?

There was a creak that sounded like the door of the plant house opening. Laney pushed herself on to the fence and tried to swing her other leg across. She hung for a moment, gripping on to the top of the wood with both hands. Now she was stuck. Great.

"Just swing yourself over," hissed Claudia.

Laney flung herself over, slid down the other side of the fence and landed in a crumpled heap. Claudia shook with silent laughter as she dragged Laney up and pulled her into the undergrowth.

"Stop laughing!" said Laney.

"Shh! Just stay still for a minute," Claudia whispered back.

Laney froze. She couldn't hear anything or see anyone following.

"It's all right. They didn't come outside," said Claudia at last, straightening up.

"How do you know they've gone?" said Laney.

"I'm a Greytail. Our senses are sharper than any other tribe's. I can hear and smell things you can't."

"Lucky you." Laney brushed dead leaves off her T-shirt.

"You wouldn't say that if you had to walk past the boys' changing room after they've had PE." Claudia wrinkled her nose. "It's so gross!"

"I don't need super senses to know that." Laney's head suddenly ached and she leaned against a tree.

She was worried about the way that Gwen had got rid of her. "Will people be happy that I've, you know, changed into a faerie?" she asked.

"Course they will. It's just…" Claudia screwed her face up. "You're twelve. Everyone was sure by now that you didn't have proper faerie magic. And now, suddenly, here you are."

"How old were you when you changed then? Did yours happen on your birthday?"

"No, it wasn't my birthday. I found out when I was about five, but I think I always knew in a way. Tom was always talking to the cats in front of me so it was pretty obvious."

"Tom can talk to cats?" asked Laney.

"Yeah, we all can – all of us in the Greytail tribe," said Claudia.

Laney thought of Claudia's brother – seventeen-year-old football-loving Tom. It seemed so weird that he had this whole side she didn't know about. "So it usually happens when you're younger than twelve?"

"Much younger."

Laney's heart sank. She couldn't even do something weird like becoming a faerie in a normal kind of way.

A light rain began to fall gently on their heads, soaking into their clothes.

"Ugh! Laney, stop it," said Claudia. "I hate getting

wet. I told you that."

"What?" Laney stared round. The rain was only falling in a small circle, which happened to be exactly where they were standing. It was her. She was making it rain.

"You're seriously going to have to stop it," Claudia told her. "You can't go round making it rain everywhere."

"I wasn't trying to make it happen," snapped Laney. "It just did!" The rain got heavier, pelting them with large drops.

"Laney!" screeched Claudia.

Laney raced away up the road, leaving the rain shower and Claudia behind.

She slowed down after she turned into Beacon Way, passing the entrance to The Cattery, the crescent-shaped road where Claudia and her family lived. This time she wasn't surprised to see a few odd-looking houses among the row of normal ones. From a distance it looked as if Claudia's house had leopard-print walls. Laney blinked and walked on.

She couldn't help thinking that she was even more of a screw-up as a faerie than before she'd changed. First she'd got herself into trouble at school and then she'd turned the river red.

She climbed the hill and saw Mrs Mottle and Mrs Hughes standing and chatting in the street. There were no gold rings in their eyes, which meant that they couldn't see any change in hers either. They were human. As she got closer, she heard bits of their conversation.

"And now there's a big patch of red in the river," Mrs Mottle told her neighbour. "I talked to Mr Lionhart down at the pet shop about it and he went very quiet."

"I bet it's a chemical spill. Someone should tell the council about it," said Mrs Hughes. "Did you see that big red moon last night? It gave me quite a shiver."

A crowd of white petals flew down from the sky and dive-bombed Mrs Mottle. Laney held her breath but Mrs Mottle didn't even blink. The sprites swept on past her ear and flew off with a tinkle of laughter. Then they came round for a second time, flying right between the two women.

"Oh dear, it's getting a bit windy, isn't it?" said Mrs Mottle, oblivious to the tiny pale things dancing past her nose. "I hope there isn't going to be another storm."

As Laney went past, Mrs Hughes whispered something and Mrs Mottle nodded. She replied in a low murmur that Laney could still hear. "My Craig told me that she broke a water fountain at school yesterday. She's turning into quite a little troublemaker."

Laney sped up, scared that any second she might make it rain on them – or something worse. She hurried down Oldwing Rise and her stomach turned over when she reached her house. The effect was quite faint, but it was definitely there – a dappled blue light played across the walls as if the whole house was underwater. Maybe becoming a Mist faerie had changed her house too.

Kim's car was gone, which probably meant that she and Toby had gone shopping. Her dad would be out with his work mate, Simon, fixing somebody's water pipes. She let herself in, went to the fridge and poured some juice. Her head was still pounding. She gulped some of the drink and tried to calm down.

The back door slammed. "Laney?" her dad called.

"I'm in the kitchen," said Laney. He must have been out in the back garden.

"Where have you been? I was looking for you." He stopped in the doorway. "I need to talk to you."

Oh great. He was still cross about the candles yesterday, which meant he'd want a long serious talk. She felt as if it was written on her forehead: *I have a huge secret. I'm a Mist faerie.* But of course he couldn't know.

"I went out for a walk," Laney said, and her stomach rumbled, reminding her that she hadn't even had any breakfast yet.

Faerie Tribes

"You shouldn't have asked Kim to borrow those candles yesterday. You know I don't like them." Her dad leaned against the door frame, his face hidden in shadow.

Laney's shoulders tensed. "I would have been careful with them." She knew she shouldn't bother arguing. He wouldn't understand.

She glanced at him and then lowered her glass. She still couldn't see him properly because the sun was shining into her eyes. But there was something about the way he was standing. He was so still he hardly even seemed to be breathing.

"What's the matter?" Laney's heart thumped. Claudia had told her humans couldn't see the change in her eyes.

"When did this happen?" Her dad's voice was hoarse.

"What do you mean?" She was playing for time now. The glass slipped a little between her fingers, so she gripped it tighter.

Her dad stepped forwards out of the shadows and looked at her with bright, gold-ringed eyes. "When did you become a faerie?"

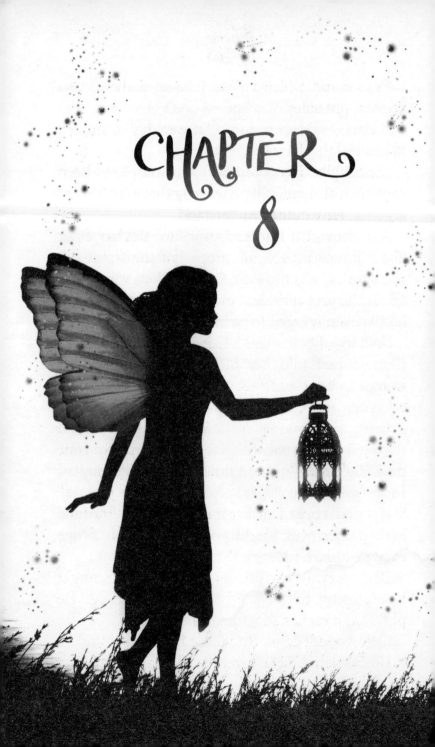

CHAPTER

8

Laney's mind whirled. "You're one of them! You knew about all of it!"

"Laney," said her dad. "Answer my question. When did this happen?"

"Last night." Her face grew red. "And you've been keeping it all a secret – pretending that everything's normal. Why didn't you tell me?"

And now the pieces began to slot together like a jigsaw puzzle. The power of the tribes ran in families. Claudia and her brother were both Greytails, probably their parents were too. Fletcher and his family were Thorns. And her home already looked like a house that belonged to a Mist faerie.

Of course he was one of them. After all, he fixed water pipes and stuff for his job. He was probably using his power over water all the time.

"Why didn't you tell me this was going to happen to me – tell me I was going to get these powers one day? I broke the water fountain in school yesterday. I touched the tap and it just exploded everywhere." She couldn't help staring at him and hating the look of his golden eyes. She'd always thought he had blue eyes, just like hers. Now that was just a lie too.

"I'm sorry. I began to think your powers might be emerging, but I hoped that it was nothing." He put a hand on her shoulder. "Are you OK?"

Laney nodded, her throat too tight to speak.

He hesitated. "Has everything that's happened

been to do with water?"

"Yes, everything. Isn't that… I mean, aren't you the same?"

"Yes, I am." An odd look passed across his face, half sad and half happy. "I meant to tell you about all of this, one day. But then you didn't Awaken and I thought perhaps you never would. Twelve years old is quite late to change. The powers of each tribe run in families but some people don't have faerie magic even if they come from faerie parents. It's rare, but it happens."

They come from faerie parents…

Laney's heart jolted painfully. "So Mum was a faerie too?"

Her dad rubbed his forehead. "Laney…"

A car door slammed outside and keys jangled.

"Hello! We're back!" called Kim, carrying a bunch of shopping bags through the front door. "Are you all right?" She looked from Laney's face to her dad's. "You look really serious."

Laney was half afraid to look at her stepmum. But when she did she found that Kim's eyes were the same greeny-grey they'd always been. Kim was a human.

"We're fine." Mr Rivers smiled. "Just…talking."

"There are some more shopping bags in the car," said Kim. "Could one of you get them for me?" She went back outside to fetch Toby.

"I know this must be a shock," said Mr Rivers quietly after she'd gone. "But Kim doesn't know and she mustn't know. It's safer that way."

Laney nodded, but she wondered who it was really safer for.

Her dad went to help with the shopping bags and she escaped upstairs. Everything in her room felt like it was from another time. She looked around at all her stuff, things she'd bought, old toys and magazines. None of it mattered now. All this time, there had been this huge thing waiting to happen.

She slumped down on her bed. What if her mum had been a faerie too? She was sure her dad had been just about to say so. Her mum had been a faerie but Kim wasn't. What did that mean?

She took a photo album out of a drawer in her bedside table and flicked to the front. Her mum had died when she was two. She'd developed an illness. That was all Laney really knew and she didn't remember much more. Sometimes she had flashes of memory – a little garden at the bottom of a huge hill, or crowding round a fireplace in the winter with tall flames leaping up the chimney.

In the photos her mum's eyes were brown. But maybe faerie eyes didn't show up in photographs.

So why had her dad kept it such a secret? Didn't she have a right to know?

She lingered over her favourite picture. It showed

Laney as a baby being held by her mum. They were both laughing. Her mum had short brown hair. Her dad must have been taking the photo.

She closed the album and shoved it back in the drawer. Her dad had thought she had no powers. He'd thought she would never become a faerie. Maybe that was why he didn't bother to tell her anything. But now that she'd changed, he didn't seem proud of her at all.

There was a knock and her dad came in. "I just wanted to check that you're OK." He closed the door behind him. "I didn't tell you about the faerie world because I left it behind long ago. I don't go to their meetings or anything. I just didn't want to any more."

Laney's forehead creased. "But why? Was it after Mum died?"

Her dad struggled with the words. "Yes, that had…a lot to do with it. I had you to think about and I believed it was better to keep you away from it all. You see, there are these different tribes—"

"I know about the tribes already," Laney cut in.

Mr Rivers frowned. "Well, that's…good, I guess. But you must be careful not to get involved with them. It would be best if you kept away from them completely."

"Dad! These are people I know. Claudia's a Greytail and she's OK."

"You've got to try and understand. They're not to be trusted." Her dad's voice rose, then he stopped and carried on in a whisper. "We had a life and a home before they interfered."

"Do you mean…when we lived in a house at the bottom of a hill? I think I remember a little bit."

Her dad's face closed up. "It was a long time ago. What you need to know is that we had to leave because of the tribes, because of their fighting." He took a deep breath. "And you need to know about the faerie rings. Don't go too near them; they're dangerous."

"Why? What do they do?"

"They're gateways to the Otherworld and they will suck you in if you go too close." Her dad looked as if he was about to say more, but he broke off. Beneath the sound of Toby playing downstairs there was something else…a rhythmic tapping that was coming closer.

Mr Rivers stared out of Laney's window. "Not now! He can't have found out that fast!"

Laney got up to look.

A man with enormous shoulders and grey hair came slowly down Oldwing Rise with his walking stick tapping on the ground. He looked up at the window, as if he had heard Mr Rivers' words, and smiled.

"Who's that?" Laney didn't like the man's smile. It

hadn't reached his eyes.

"That's Peter Stingwood. He's a Thorn and he lives over in Gillforth."

At once, Laney wondered if this was all about the river turning red. "Dad? I made a mistake when I went out last night. I stepped into the river and part of it turned this horrible red colour." Laney had a sudden vivid recollection of the shadowy figure that had terrified her so much. She tried to shake off the twist of fear that returned with the memory. "I just got spooked in the dark – I think it was the red moon, making everything look all strange…"

"What's that?" Her dad turned white. "Did you say there was a red moon *last night*?"

"Yes, it was a full moon and it was quite a deep red," Laney's voice faltered.

"Why didn't I see it? I didn't know…"

Laney blinked. That was almost the same as what Gwen had said. Her stomach turned over. She'd never seen her dad look so worried before.

The tapping sound of the walking stick came from the front path. Then came the knock at the door.

"Hello, Peter." Kim's voice came from the hallway. "How are you? Did you come to see Robert? It's not a plumbing disaster, I hope?"

Laney and her dad listened for the muttered reply from downstairs.

"Dad? Is everything all right?" said Laney.

"You'll have to come downstairs and meet Peter Stingwood." Her dad's voice was grim. "But leave the talking to me. You don't know what you're dealing with."

CHAPTER
9

Laney followed her dad downstairs.

Mr Stingwood turned to look at her appraisingly with deep gold-ringed eyes. Laney couldn't believe how broad he was. He seemed to fill the room.

"Hello, Robert," he said. "And this must be your daughter. How fast they grow up these days!" His bushy eyebrows drew downwards.

"What do you need, Peter?" said Mr Rivers.

"Ah, it's just a simple pipe repair, I'm sure." Mr Stingwood glanced at Kim.

"Come out to the garage and I'll look out some tools." Mr Rivers held open the door, his face drawn tight.

"Very kind of you." Mr Stingwood manoeuvred his huge bulk through the doorway using his dark-mahogany stick.

As he turned, Laney noticed the same silvery marks on the backs of his hands that she'd seen on Gwen's. She went to follow them, and as she passed the sink, the bowl full of washing-up water started to bubble. Luckily no one saw except Toby, sitting in his high chair.

"Bubbly water, Laney," he said.

Laney put a finger to her lips.

When they reached the garage, the manner of both men changed completely. Mr Stingwood leaned his walking stick against the wall and towered over Laney's dad.

"What is it, Peter?" said Mr Rivers. "You know I want nothing to do with tribe business."

"You don't, but what about her?" said Mr Stingwood coldly. "She's Awake now, so she needs to be taken to see a Mist Elder."

"Who's that?" asked Laney.

"Leave this to me, Laney," said her dad. "We're not having anything to do with the rest of you. So you can go back and tell that to the Elders."

Stingwood's eyes hardened. "*You* may not want anything to do with faerie business, but *she* became our business when she Awoke on the night of the Wolf Moon. You know what that means."

Mr Rivers paled. "That's not what the prophecy says. It doesn't say *Awaken at the red moon.*"

"It's close enough," replied Stingwood.

"You're making up reasons to interfere—" began Mr Rivers.

"She turned the river red. Did she tell you that?" Stingwood glared at Mr Rivers. "Is that a normal thing for a Mist faerie to do?"

Mr Rivers was silent.

"What do you want me to do?" said Laney.

"You must meet with the Elders and we will need to see a demonstration of your Mist power." Stingwood watched her with narrow eyes. "And after the test we will decide if it's safe that you remain here in Skellmore."

"No!" said her dad. "You want to perform the Seeing Thread on her. That's a dangerous and painful thing to do. I'll never let her go to be tested by all of you. Just because you and that Mist Elder, Arthur Puddlewick—"

"Arthur Puddlewick is dead. He died yesterday," said Stingwood sharply.

"But that doesn't mean... You can't assume that has anything to do with Laney; she didn't even know him. Anyway, he was quite an old man," said Laney's dad.

Stingwood waved away the objection with a dismissive hand. "In the circumstances, everything is suspicious – Awakenings, deaths, everything. And she *must* come to be tested."

"Never!" Mr Rivers squared his shoulders, even though Laney had never seen him so pale. "I shall never let a child of mine go through the Seeing Thread. And if you come here again I shall throw you out."

"You would be wise not to get in our way," said Stingwood. "We will return." He picked up his stick and left.

"What's the Seeing Thread?" whispered Laney.

Her dad shook his head. "It's horrible. It's a way to judge someone, to find out how strong their power is or whether they've committed a spell crime. It was done a lot in the old days. Some faeries never fully recovered." He hurried out of the garage and back towards the house, nearly tripping over Toby who was coming out to play.

Laney followed more slowly.

"Girl," called Stingwood quietly. He had stopped just beyond the wall of the next-door garden, where he couldn't be seen from their house.

Laney walked down the front path towards him.

"Your father is foolish," said Stingwood. "It is true that the Seeing Thread is dangerous, but it needs to be done. He cannot stand in our way and if he does, we will test all his children instead of just you. Is that what you want?"

Laney's eyes flew to where Toby was playing, wheeling his ride-on car up and down the front path. This was her fault, not Toby's. She couldn't let him suffer this horrible Thread thing. "Where do you want me to go?"

He pointed his walking stick and the tree next to them leaned away, as if it was afraid. "Come to Hobbin Forest at eleven thirty tonight. The Elders will meet you there."

"Will Gwen be there – I mean, Mrs Whitefern?"

"All the Elders will be there. Tell no one about this." Stingwood turned, and as he tapped his way back down the lane he added one more thing over his shoulder. "Be on time, otherwise we'll come back here for your brother too."

Laney felt as if she'd swallowed a lump of ice. But she couldn't let them have Toby; this was nothing to do with him.

"Oh! Has Peter gone?" Kim came out of the house. "I was just going to ask him if he wanted a cup of tea."

Laney turned away so that Kim couldn't see her fear. "Yes, he's gone," she managed to say.

Tonight she was going to be tested. The thought of it weighed on her chest so much that she could hardly breathe.

Laney spent the rest of the day desperately trying to make her Mist powers work. If the faerie Elders were going to do some sort of test on her, she thought she should practise as much as she could. So she took a bowl of water to her bedroom and stared at it for a long, long time. She managed to get a few drops to rise up from the bowl and float in the air.

At last, exhausted, she collapsed on her bed. Considering the amount of damage she'd caused to the school water fountain, and the rain shower she'd made that morning, it was surprisingly hard to get the water to do anything. It was much easier to do it all by accident. She glanced at her gold-ringed eyes in the mirror. She just hoped she could make her powers work tonight.

* * *

It felt like a long wait until the sun went down.

Her dad turned to her at teatime while Kim was taking some dishes out to the kitchen. "Don't worry about Stingwood. Just leave those people to me."

"What's the prophecy he was talking about?" said Laney. "Is it something to do with the red moon?"

Her dad hesitated. "Yes, it's all to do with that, but it's just nonsense and you don't have to worry about it. I don't want them dragging you into it."

Laney knew he wanted to protect her but she had to meet the Elders. It was her they wanted and if she could prove to them that there was nothing wrong with her, then maybe they would leave her family alone after that.

At eleven o'clock she opened her window wide. She knew she wouldn't get out of the front door without her dad noticing, but if she could use her wings then she might be able to get out by flying.

She climbed on to the window ledge, closed her eyes and tried to clear her mind. It took several minutes until she felt what she was hoping for. There was a swish of air behind her and smooth pale wings curved open from her back. She touched them, amazed all over again. Then she looked down at the lane below.

There was one slight problem with her plan...she

didn't really know how to fly.

Maybe if she made sure her wings were spread wide she could at least glide down to the ground without hurting herself.

She pressed her lips together tightly. This was it.

Launching herself upwards, she spread out her arms and her wings opened too. She sailed over the plum tree by the front gate, lifted for a moment by the wind. But the ground zoomed upwards and she put her hands out to protect herself before hurtling straight into the churchyard wall on the other side of the lane.

She picked herself up and examined her scratches and scrapes. Vowing not to try that again until she knew how to do it properly, she ran down the lane. She didn't stop till she'd passed the last house on the edge of the village.

It was weird walking along with wings. Even though they were light, they bumped against her back a little, and now and then a gust of wind caught them and lifted her off her feet. She closed her eyes to tell them to go. Even though she was outside Skellmore, it would be better to get rid of them. If she was seen like this she'd have a hard time explaining it.

But with her eyes closed, her mind filled up with terror. She told herself it was just because she'd shut her eyes in the middle of the countryside.

She opened them again. The footpath in front of her ran down to a narrow stream that joined the larger river half a mile further along. Even though nothing moved in the darkness, her skin prickled.

Giving in to instinct, she ran down the footpath and through the fields, not slowing down until her panic subsided. As she reached the edge of Hobbin Forest, a bright full moon rose above the trees. Seeing its round white face made Laney wonder again why it had looked so red the night before.

She shivered, noticing that her wings had suddenly disappeared and she was back in human form again. She wished she could make the change happen when she wanted it to.

The church clock struck the half hour. She was meant to be meeting the faerie Elders right now. She took a deep breath and plunged under the canopy of the dark trees.

CHAPTER 10

Laney had no idea where in the forest she was supposed to be meeting the Elders. She struggled on through the trees and their low branches scraped her arms.

"Stop," said an icy voice. A bright light blinded her.

She shielded her face. She was in a clearing, with Mr Stingwood and a lady with cold-looking eyes. Mr Stingwood didn't have his walking stick with him this time and the way he strode forwards made Laney wonder if he'd ever really needed it.

The bright light came from a white orb that he was holding. He let it float upwards to hang in the air above them. "Let us begin," he said, and with a sweep of his hand he made the trees and bushes around the edge of the clearing grow together into a tightly knitted thicket set with savage thorns.

Laney gasped. She was stuck inside a prison of branches. There would be no getting in or out. When she turned back, Stingwood and the lady had changed to faerie form. The air glowed white around them and the silvery marks on Stingwood's hands were bright. Their wings were folded behind them.

"But where's Mrs Whitefern?" said Laney.

Stingwood ignored her. "This is Miss Reed." He pointed to the lady with the icicle eyes. "She will be conducting your test. She's standing in for Mr

Puddlewick, who used to be the Elder of your tribe."

"Are you ready to begin?" Miss Reed's eyes drilled into Laney.

Laney's heart thumped. She felt less ready than ever before.

"Wait!" The voice that spoke sounded far away. Then the woven thicket rustled.

"Peter, you must let us through!"

Laney's heart lifted. That sounded like Gwen's voice. Surely Gwen would help her.

Stingwood frowned but waved a hand to let a tunnel open in the tightly woven branches. Two faeries came through. The tangle of thorns shut instantly behind them. Gwen looked graceful in her faerie form despite her plump frame and lined face. She wore a gauzy scarf around her head and short wings glistened behind her.

Laney noticed with a jolt that the other figure was Claudia's mum. Mrs Lionhart was small, but her dark wings and fierce eyes gave her an air of power. She stared at Laney with open curiosity.

The air in the clearing buzzed with magic. Standing among these four powerful faeries made Laney wish she could find a way through the thicket and sneak back home.

"You should not have shut me out like that, Peter," said Gwen sharply. "I am a Thorn Elder too."

Stingwood bowed. "My *deepest* apologies," he

said silkily.

"This must be done with the utmost care," Gwen went on. "Testing someone who's only just Awakened – we've never done anything like this before."

"We haven't performed the Seeing Thread on a grown faerie for several years," said Mrs Lionhart.

"There hasn't been a red moon before," replied Stingwood. "Not in the last twelve years. The girl has Awoken at a time of bad omens. We must put maudlin feelings aside and do our duty."

Laney didn't like being called "the girl" very much. "Why is everyone so worried about the moon being red last night?" she said.

"This is not the time or place to explain faerie lore to you." Mr Stingwood's bushy eyebrows lowered. "Do not speak unless you are asked to."

"If it's something to do with me, I'd like to know." Laney was amazed at how brave she sounded. She folded her arms tight to stop him seeing how much she was shaking.

"See these markings?" Mr Stingwood showed her the silvery marks on his hands. "These are the signs of a faerie Elder. If you cross me, you will regret it."

"Peter! She's only just Awakened." Gwen turned to Laney. "There's a legend among faeries about a child who will be born at the time of a red moon. That kind of moon – called a Wolf Moon – has always brought bad luck. No one knows for sure what the prophecy means, but—"

"Greytails don't believe in it anyway," said Mrs Lionhart fiercely. "It's a lot of silly superstition."

Stingwood drew himself up to his full height and pointed at Laney. "How can you stand there calling it superstition when we have a girl here who Awakened on the night of the Wolf Moon? If she shows signs of unnatural power we must send her to the Faerie Council immediately."

Laney's heart began to race. Her dad had told her not to worry about the red moon prophecy, but that was the main reason she was being tested. Becoming a faerie on the night of the red moon had made people suspicious of her.

"But the prophecy says the child will be *born* under that moon, not Awaken," said Gwen. "When is your birthday, Laney?"

"July the fifteenth," Laney said automatically. "Yesterday."

"You see?" Stingwood's face darkened. "She had her birthday yesterday on the night of the Wolf Moon."

"Yes, but she can't have been *born* under a red moon because there's never been one in the month of July before," said Gwen.

Stingwood glared, but didn't argue.

"May I suggest we start the test?" Miss Reed cut

in. "Come here, child."

"Will it hurt?" Laney walked reluctantly to the edge of the forest pool where Miss Reed stood.

"For the first part I simply require you to show me what you can do." She clicked her fingers and the white orb floated closer to them, shining down on the pool and turning it into a dark mirror. The wind blew and the leaves on the edge of the clearing rustled. Laney thought she saw something move on the other side of the thicket, but then it was gone.

"We'll start with something simple," said Miss Reed. "Raise a single drop of water from the pool up to at least waist height."

Laney focused on the pool and tried to concentrate. One drop, just one drop, she begged silently. The water stirred a little, but no drop appeared. Her cheeks grew hot. She tried again, putting every tiny bit of her willpower into making the water move, but it made no difference.

"Oh dear! Finding it difficult, are we?" Miss Reed's eyebrows rose. "Let's try something else. Turn part of the pool into ice. You may touch the water if you need to."

Laney crouched down by the pool and put both hands in the water. She shut her eyes this time and tried to imagine the pond turning hard and white as a layer of ice stretched across it. She heard a faint hiss and opened her eyes. The water hadn't changed at all. The faerie Elders were looking at her with various degrees of surprise, pity and disdain.

"Are you sure she isn't cheating?" Stingwood asked Miss Reed, who shrugged. "Well, there's one way to find out." From his pocket he drew a silver thread almost too thin to see. His dark-green wings flared out, as if he was pleased by what was to come.

"The Seeing Thread allows us to see the truth of things," Gwen explained to Laney. "We can use it to see exactly how much Mist power you really have. In the old days it was made of hemp, but it can be made of anything as long as it's been dipped into a faerie ring."

"This one is spider silk, by the look of it. We must prime it with the power we're searching for." Miss Reed took the fragile-looking silver thread and plunged it into the pool. It came out decorated with water drops that gleamed white in the light from the orb.

"Hurry up, for goodness' sake," said Mrs Lionhart. "I don't want to be out here all night."

"Hold the girl still," said Stingwood, taking back the thread.

Miss Reed took Laney's arms and held them behind her back.

"You must remain absolutely still, Laney," said Gwen. "The whole procedure becomes dangerous if you start moving."

Laney felt sick. She glanced at the tightly closed walls of the thicket all around her. She had to remember that she was doing this for Toby, to keep him safe.

Stingwood stood close to her, widening the loop and holding it over her head. As he brought the string down around her, a searing pain began at the top of her forehead and worked down over her face, matching the pace of the string. Longing to move but knowing that she mustn't, she clenched her fists.

The Elders were speaking to each other but their voices were muffled by the pain in her head. Stingwood carried on lowering the thread, past her neck and over her shoulders to her middle. Suddenly the loop was broken. Miss Reed let go of Laney's hands and she fell to the ground, the agony inside her fading.

"Laney!" Gwen bent over her. "You were so brave, my dear. I'm sorry you had to go through that." She picked some pale feathery leaves from a plant growing near the trunk of a tree. "Smell this feverfew. It will help a little."

She crushed the leaves between the palms of her hands and gave them to Laney, who breathed them in and instantly felt a lot better.

"Tell me the results," Stingwood commanded. "How much Mist power does she have?"

"She failed to raise even a single drop of water from the pool. She has a tiny amount of Mist power and the Seeing Thread confirms that," said Miss Reed. "I do *not* think we need to fear this child as the next evil faerie of our time. It's most likely that she didn't Awaken until the age of twelve because she's barely a faerie at all."

"But what about how she turned the river water red?" said Mrs Lionhart sharply. "That seems real enough."

"It was probably a one-off that happened because the child had just Awoken. A sudden burst of energy around the time of Awakening has been known before, but that doesn't mean she'll carry on being powerful," said Miss Reed smoothly. "We all know that the father ignores faerie ways and has married a human. This is a family where the power is dying out and that is fine by me. She should not join the Mist tribe. There is no room in our clan for weaklings."

Laney met her cold eyes. "But aren't I already in the Mist tribe? I mean, my power is over…water…" She trailed off. She hadn't exactly shown them she had control over water.

"You are a Mist, I suppose," said Miss Reed. "But no one is taught how to use their full power without an invitation from their tribe and I shall not be recommending you for training."

Laney felt hollow inside. She'd failed the test. She hadn't been able to show them anything.

"I find it impossible to believe that she is so weak." Stingwood pointed his finger in Laney's face. "We must be absolutely sure. Hold her arms whilst I use the Seeing Thread again." His eyes gleamed as he reassembled the loop in the spider silk.

"No, that is enough. No more." Gwen spread her wings and the air around her blazed with light. Stingwood's eyes narrowed. "Don't oppose me on this, Peter. Your Thorn spells are strong, but you have never tried them against mine."

"The test is done," said Mrs Lionhart fiercely. "Leave the child alone."

Stingwood puffed out his chest angrily, but before he could speak the branches at the bottom of the thicket snapped and a hole appeared. A scuffling came from behind the bushes, followed by a low stuttering snarl.

"Hobgobbits!" said Gwen. "Your wall of thorns won't stop them, Peter!"

"We shall *not* be interrupted by those low creatures!" snapped Stingwood. "We will get rid of them and carry on."

A dozen more holes appeared in the thicket and a squat shape that was little more than waist high rushed straight at them. Laney tried to dodge, but the growling thing caught her by the ankles and knocked her over. She had a close-up view of its matted fur and sharp teeth.

"Ow!" she yelled, as it drew blood from her arm with its claws. She kicked out, managing to free herself and scramble up.

More of the creatures entered the clearing in a strange lurching kind of run. Miss Reed was firing ice bolts at them while Stingwood grabbed two by their arms and hurled them at the thicket wall.

"Quick, Laney! Go now while the other Elders are busy," Gwen said into her ear. "Run!"

"What are those things?" gasped Laney.

"Hobgobbits. They're nasty little things and they hate faeries. We'll get rid of them. Now, go."

"There's no way out!"

Gwen touched her shoulders and Laney felt the rush of power as her wings unfolded behind her back. "Fly!" said Gwen.

CHAPTER
11

Laney took a deep breath and launched into the air. Her wings snagged on the branches but she struggled on and flew over the thicket before bumping down to the ground again. Then she ran and ran until she'd left the hobgobbits and the Elders far behind. The terror of the night lessened a little. She didn't know whether she was happier to get away from Stingwood or those creatures.

She pushed back the wisps of hair that had fallen over her eyes. Now that she thought about it, it wasn't very hard to choose. Horrible as the hobgobbits were, with their growling and their pointed teeth, she'd rather face them than Stingwood any day.

She slowed down at the edge of Skellmore and spent a while trying to make her faerie form disappear. Why hadn't she been able to use her Mist power in front of the Elders? She felt so stupid.

At last she managed to change back to human form. Then she hurried down the High Street, only stopping when she heard the sound of laughter. A few kids from school were hanging out next to the minimart and all of them had gold-ringed eyes.

"Hey, Laney!" Jessie walked up to Laney and looked her up and down.

Laney's heart sank. So Jessie was a faerie too. Great.

Jessie faked a theatrical yawn. "I heard you'd Awoken *at last*. It must have been really boring waiting for *so long*."

The kids behind Laney sniggered.

Jessie's eyes gleamed as she sensed Laney's discomfort. "So now that you're a Mist like me, you need to stop being such a freak and do *something* about your hair." Her eyes swept over Laney's clothes and she curled her lip.

"We're in the same tribe?" Laney hadn't thought her heart could sink any lower.

"Only if you really are a Mist faerie, and right now I really doubt that. And you can't hang around with Claudia like you did this morning," said Jessie. "Mist faeries don't make friends with Greytails."

"Why?" said Laney.

"Because they're Greytails, stupid!" said Jessie. "They hang around with smelly animals. Didn't you realise what the stink was?" Right on cue, the kids behind her laughed again.

"I'll show you what a real Mist faerie looks like." Jessie walked round the corner of the minimart, out of sight of the houses. The air shimmered as she changed into faerie form and stretched out violet wings. She swept her curly dark hair over her shoulders. "I heard that you can't actually control your powers at all. What is the point of a faerie that can't do that?" She leaned forwards. "And I was there just now, hidden behind the trees. I saw you fail the test and now they'll never invite you to start training." She stepped back, her eyes alight with triumph.

"You were there?" Laney stared at her, disbelieving.

"You don't deserve to be a Mist tribe member anyway," said Jessie. "Not after the things you've done. Even when we were little I knew there was something wrong with you."

"Shut up, Jessie."

"It's probably your dad's fault. I bet freakiness runs in your family."

Laney's fists balled and she changed to faerie form instantly. As her anger rose she felt her wings begin to beat.

Jessie rolled her eyes. "Ooh, wings! Big wow! I bet you can't even fly properly."

The other faerie kids gave a cheer as Jessie swooped into the air and flew away across the fields.

Hot with anger, Laney flew straight after her.

"Face it, Laney!" Jessie yelled back at her. "There's something wrong with you and you'll never be one of us!"

Laney accelerated through the air. She would catch Jessie and make her sorry for being mean about her dad. She started to gain on her, but Jessie swung round and, seeing Laney so close, stretched out her hand. A cloud of hail with ice the size of tennis balls beat down on Laney, who put her hands over her head to protect herself. One hailstone hit her on the side of the face and she fell, spiralling downwards through the air. She hit the ground and lay there, unable to move.

"Serves you right, freak girl," called Jessie, and with a swish of purple wings she flew away.

Laney lay there for a while, while the balls of ice melted around her. Every muscle in her body hurt and she didn't feel like she'd ever move again. What hurt even more was that some of what Jessie said was true. She had failed the test and Miss Reed had told her that she'd never become a proper member of the Mist tribe.

The stars became brighter and she heard foxes barking in the forest. Claudia's face loomed over her, making her jump. "What are you doing?"

Laney tried to sit up. "I had a…row with Jessie. Then she hit me with these hailstones."

Claudia raised her eyebrows. "So much for people in the same tribe sticking together. She's never really liked you, has she?"

"I guess not." Laney got up and brushed the half-melted ice off her dress. "I need to learn how to do that hailstone thing. Then if she tries it again I'll get her back."

"That's the spirit," said Claudia.

Laney looked at her, noticing for the first time that she was in human form. "How did you know I was here?"

"I didn't. I was just wandering around a bit and talking to the cats. They're still freaked out by the red moon last night, same as the grown-ups are. But at least the river's back to its normal colour."

"It's not red any more?" Laney felt relieved. At least everyone would stop being upset about what she'd done.

"Yeah, don't do that again. It looked gross." Claudia paused. "Why are you out here anyway?"

"I had to meet the Elders in Hobbin Forest. They wanted to test my Mist powers because of the red moon." Laney clenched her hands for a moment, remembering how much it had hurt.

"Weird," said Claudia. "They're really stressed out about this red moon thing. But us Greytails don't believe in that kind of stuff. Did you say my mum was there?"

Laney nodded. "I didn't know she was an Elder."

They began walking across the field together. "She's the only Greytail Elder in the village, worse luck, and she never lets me forget it. So what kind of test was it?"

"They used this thread. They made it into a loop and put it around me—"

"The Seeing Thread?" Claudia's eyes nearly popped. "No way! That's serious stuff. They use it for judging spell crimes and things like that, but

I've never heard of it being used on someone young before. Does it hurt as much as it's supposed to?"

"It was horrible but it was over quickly, I guess." Laney didn't add that she'd gone to save Toby from having to go through it. She was sure Gwen wouldn't have wanted Toby tested, but Stingwood was definitely nasty enough to do it.

"Did they find anything?" said Claudia.

"Not really. I'm not supposed to be the greatest Mist faerie of the century or anything."

Claudia shot Laney a sideways look, her eyes thoughtful.

They came to the footpath that ran behind the village. From there, they turned up Oldwing Rise and stopped outside Laney's house.

"I'll never get back up there." Laney looked in despair at her open window. "I don't want to wake my dad up."

"I can help you get back in. Just give me a minute." Claudia fiddled with the front door for a moment and it opened noiselessly. "It's an old Greytail trick," she said. "They don't have cat burglars for nothing. Isn't that right, Dizzy?"

Miaow! A small black cat ran over and circled round Claudia's ankles.

"Do all Greytails like cats as much as you?" said Laney.

"Course they do! Cats are one of the few animals

that can see faerie magic. That makes them special. Go, and I'll lock it again behind you."

Laney crept upstairs and into her bedroom. Her back still felt sore from where she had hit the ground, but more than anything she felt angry – with Jessie and with the icy Miss Reed. She looked in the mirror and a pair of gold-ringed eyes glared back. So what if twelve years old was freakishly late to Awaken? She would show them all. She would become just as good at faerie magic as anyone in Skellmore.

CHAPTER 12

Laney dreamed that she was falling. Darkness rushed past her. She stretched out her wings and tried to fly, but they barely slowed the speed of her fall. Then a black shape flew overhead, blotting out the stars.

At last her wings began to work and she swooped down over Oldwing Rise, looking for somewhere to hide. Behind her she heard the sweep of massive wings. She landed in the churchyard and crouched down behind a gravestone, fear creeping up her spine. She couldn't see the black shape any more but she could feel that it was close. Even the trees next to the church wall seemed to shiver.

The stars overhead were clear and bright, but something moved in the corner of Laney's eye. She turned her head, slowly, towards the far corner. There was a small pond, fenced off from the rest of the churchyard to keep children safe. A black shape bent down over the surface of the pond and spread out its wings.

It was the same dark shape she'd seen by the river on the night of the red moon. She was sure of it. She hadn't seen any wings then, but it used the same horrible sliding movement. She knew she had to get away but a cold feeling crept through her, making it hard to move. The coldness grew stronger and she clasped her numb hands together.

The black shape was moving round the edge of

the pond. It bent over as if it was searching for something. It circled the pond for a long time, then with a sudden sweep of its wings it turned, knocking over part of the fence that surrounded the water. There was a loud crack as the wood splintered. Laney gasped, shocked at the proof that the figure was solid and real.

The figure scanned the churchyard, its wings spread out like a venomous bat's. Laney crouched as low as she could as it took flight and rose into the sky.

She woke up with her heart pounding.

Grateful that it was only a dream, she opened her curtains and looked at the churchyard opposite. Nothing was moving and the stars were covered by cloud. She closed the curtains tightly and lay back down in bed, wishing that she could wipe the picture of the dark figure from her mind.

When she woke up, the room was full of daylight. She got dressed and went downstairs to find her dad waiting for her. She tried to smile, but she still couldn't get used to his gold-ringed eyes.

"Morning, love," he said. "Simon and I are doing a job in town this morning and then we're driving back at lunchtime. Would you like a lift in with us? You've probably got friends there that you want to see."

Laney's heart leaped. A lift into Pennington!

Except that Steph would be on holiday by now so they wouldn't be able to meet up. "I don't know. I might just hang out here." She put some bread into the toaster and got a plate from the cupboard.

"You're not tired, are you?" Her dad paused. "Did you go out last night? I told you to leave the Elders to me. You are *not* to get involved with them. They're awful people."

"Gwen doesn't seem awful," Laney said, avoiding the question.

Her dad stiffened. "The Thorns are not to be trusted. You don't know what the faerie tribes have done in the past."

A shadow fell across the window. A black cat walked along the window ledge, glancing in at them. Her dad banged on the glass, making the cat jump down and run away across the garden. "Wretched Greytails," he muttered.

"Dad? What have the Thorns done in the past?"

Mr Rivers hesitated before he said, "You're too young to hear it."

Laney scowled. He was still treating her like a child and after everything she'd put herself through.

"You haven't answered me," said her dad. "Did you go out last night?"

"I—" Laney broke off as the front door opened and Kim came in.

"Vandals!" said Kim. "Wretched vandals!"

Simon Morden, Mr Rivers' work mate, followed her in. "Morning, everyone," he said, nearly tripping over Kim's shopping bag with his long legs.

"Morning, Simon." Mr Rivers turned to Kim. "What's wrong, love?"

Laney wasn't surprised when she saw that Simon had gold-ringed eyes. He'd worked with her dad for years, so he was likely to be a faerie too. He winked at her when Kim wasn't looking. Laney smiled back and picked her toast out of the toaster.

"It makes me so cross," said Kim, putting a loaf of bread down on the table. "I was on my way back from the minimart and some vandals must have broken a fence last night. It's completely smashed."

Laney froze in the middle of buttering her toast. A fence had been smashed, just like in her dream. "Was it in the churchyard by the pond?"

"Yes it was." Kim swung round on Laney. "What do you know about it? I hope you haven't been mucking around. I heard that you've been in trouble at school. Craig told his mum that you broke a water fountain and caused a flood in the corridors. I told them that you weren't the type to get in trouble." She gave Laney a serious look.

Laney flushed.

"That wasn't her fault," Mr Rivers said quickly. "It was just an accident, so there's no need to worry about it."

Kim took another loaf out of the carrier bag. "Well, I didn't know about any of that. You two are great ones for secrets!"

"It's such a shame about the fence," said Mr Rivers, quickly changing the subject. "It was put there to keep little children away from the water. That pond could be really dangerous."

"You expect Skellmore to be safe from that kind of vandalism," said Simon. "I hope they find the person who did it."

Laney stared down at her toast. In her head she could hear the moment when the fence splintered and she could see the terrifying black shape with its wings spread. Feeling shaky, she finished eating and decided to go out.

Simon followed her to the front door. "Hey! Well done on...you know." He grinned. "Joining the secret club, I guess. How are you finding it all so far?"

"Fine, thanks." Laney forced a smile, but the last thing she wanted to do was talk about her life with one of her dad's friends. "Er...I have to..."

"See you soon," said Simon with a final wink.

Laney hurried down the front path, relieved to get away. Checking there was no one around, she let herself into the churchyard and walked over to the pond in the corner.

Dreamlike, she touched the broken wooden bars

of the fence that circled the pond. Whatever did this was massively strong. So was it just chance that she'd dreamed of the broken fence on the same night, or had the dark shape really been here?

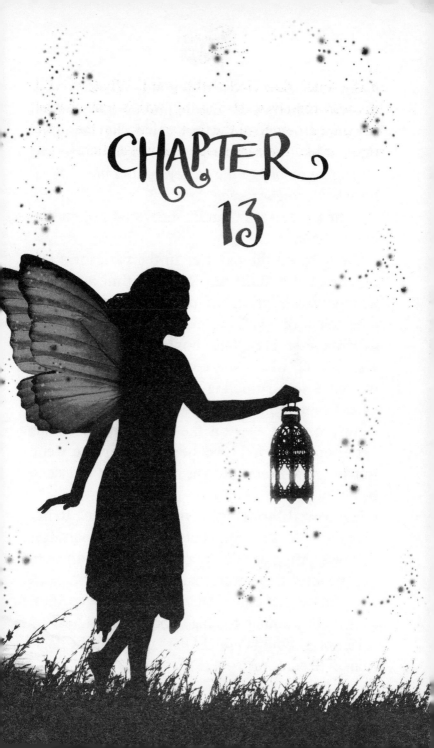

CHAPTER
13

Laney wandered down to the High Street, trying to decide whether she should find Claudia and tell her about the dream. What could she say? *Hey! Guess what I dreamed about last night? There was something spooky in the graveyard and now I think the whole thing was real!*

If she tried to tell Claudia she would just end up looking stupid.

She watched the oak tree in the park for a few minutes, but it didn't turn gold this time and there was only one group of petal-like sprites flying over the rooftops. The faerie houses still looked as strange as ever. One house on the corner of The Cattery, which was covered with dark spines, uttered a deep rumbling growl as she passed. But what Laney found hardest to get used to were the giant green cat eyes on the wall of the Lionhart Pet Shop. They followed her wherever she went, watching her every move as if she were a mouse to be pounced on.

She passed Mrs Mottle, who was chatting to her neighbour, Mrs Hughes, outside the minimart. Her dog was sitting beside her on its lead. "And would you believe, there were hailstones falling against my window last night," she said, "and a shape flew over that was much too big to be a normal owl."

Her neighbour laughed. "Perhaps it was the Eagle Man of Skellmore!"

Laney glanced at them guiltily. The thing Mrs Mottle had seen in the sky was probably her or Jessie. She would have to be more careful. She jumped as a tiger-like car zoomed past, all glowing eyes and sharp teeth. Claudia's teenage brother Tom waved from inside it. The car growled, then pounced on a chocolate wrapper and chewed it up before roaring away again.

"Is he old enough to drive now?" Laney heard Mrs Mottle say behind her. "It's a bit of an old banger, isn't it?"

Laney hid a grin. Obviously only faeries could see the tiger features. But her smile faded as Craig came out of the shop clutching some packets of sweets. "Hey, Laney!" he called. "Bust any water fountains lately? Ow!" He dropped his sweets as a large drop of water from a drainpipe on the wall hit him right between the eyes.

Laney hurried on. She'd managed to do that on purpose, so at least her Mist skills weren't totally useless.

Still wondering about her dream, she took the footpath down to the river. If she was going to practise using her Mist power it seemed like a good place to go. She stopped on the bridge and looked down at the bubbling water. It wasn't just Mist skills she needed to improve. She didn't know anything about flying and she couldn't even change into faerie form when she wanted to. Last night's transformation in front of Jessie had been easy because she was angry. Now she just had to do it without getting mad.

She closed her eyes and pictured herself with wings. But when she opened them again nothing had changed. She was still in jeans and a blue T-shirt with a tomato ketchup stain on the front.

Jessie and all the other faerie kids must think she was so stupid, not Awakening till she was twelve years old…

She shut her eyes and tried to put Jessie's mocking face out of her mind. The sound of the rushing river filled her thoughts, drawing her in. A bubbling feeling rose inside her. Something brushed against her back and a pair of translucent wings unfolded from her shoulders. She opened her eyes. Her dress was the same pale blue as before and her skin shone.

Now she just had to find a way to fly.

She crossed the bridge to reach the field on the other side. A cloud of sprites swooped over her and flew away again. The dark mass of Hobbin Forest could be seen a couple of miles away and the unmistakable glimmer of magic hung in the air above it.

Laney struggled to spread her wings. Getting them to move was like using a new muscle, like running when she'd never used her legs before. But at the same time it felt weirdly normal.

She rose on to her tiptoes and sprang into the air. Her wings took her upwards for a few seconds before she bumped back down again. She tried again and this time managed to fly a few metres along the riverbank.

She paused, listening. There was a rustling, panting sound coming from the other side of the river. She heard a voice. "Slow down, Daisy! My legs aren't as young as yours."

Laney put out her arms, trying to hide her wings from view. Mrs Mottle must be just around the bend in the footpath. She was moments from being discovered like this and there was nowhere to hide. She should never have done this in daylight.

Pushing that thought away, she shut her eyes and wished she was back in human form, but the change didn't happen.

A little long-haired dog scampered round the corner.

Laney did the only thing she could think of and dived into the river. The water closed round her like a sheet of silk and her wings moved, helping her to glide. This was easier than flying. She felt no need to breathe. This must be a Mist faerie skill – flying through the river with water wings.

Not wanting to be spotted coming back to the surface, she flew on. As her confidence grew, she turned head over heels and darted past a shoal of fish. She must have gone far enough now. Flying upwards, she peeked through the river's surface. There were fields of sheep on both sides and no one else in sight. She shot into the air and hovered there, looking at the countryside around her.

A little way off there was a hilltop crowned by a massive circular stone with a hole in the middle. As soon as she saw it she knew where she was. This was Mencladden Hill. The standing stone was from the Bronze Age and sometimes holidaymakers came to visit it in the summer. She must have flown underwater for miles to get this far from Skellmore.

She landed on the riverbank and shook the water drops off her wings. Close by she saw a dark-green circle in the grass.

A faerie ring.

She walked towards it, her stomach flipping over. Yes, it was supposed to be dangerous. But what was it? Her dad had called it a gateway to the Otherworld. Wouldn't it be great to see what was really in there?

The ring wasn't perfect. It had uneven edges, but the dark-green grass was unbroken all the way around. Inside, the grass looked completely normal, dotted with daisies and weeds. Once she was closer she could hear the faint sound of high voices singing. It made her skin tingle and she longed to hear them more clearly.

She took another step forwards.

"Laney!" A hand grabbed her shoulder, pulling her backwards.

"No!" She struggled to shake the hand off. She was close to the edge of the ring and she was sure the voices were singing just for her.

The hand kept pulling her backwards and she realised that Fletcher Thornbeam was shaking her. "Laney, stop it! You can't go in there."

Laney pushed him away furiously. "Get off, Fletcher!"

"Listen to me, will you?" Fletcher glared at her. "You've got no idea what you're doing. You've only been a faerie for five minutes. These rings are dangerous."

Laney blinked and looked away. He thought she was stupid just like Jessie did. The little girl who didn't even find out she was a faerie till she was twelve years old. Fletcher was in the year above at school. He probably thought she was a baby and this just made it official.

Suddenly she realised that they were hovering in mid-air. Fletcher was wearing a dark top and jeans, and a pair of smooth grey wings flared out behind him.

"I heard that you'd Awoken," said Fletcher. "You look…different."

Laney rolled her eyes. "Yeah? Well, I'm flying right now, so that *would* be different. You don't need to explain about the rings. I already knew about them and I was only looking anyway." She flew down to the ground and drew in her wings.

Fletcher pushed his dark fringe away from his face. "You just scared me standing there, right on the edge of it. My dad says he saw someone vanish inside one long ago. They're deadly."

Laney gazed at the ring feeling slightly sick. Suddenly it reminded her of a picture she'd seen of a black hole in space, dark and irresistible, sucking in everything around it.

Fletcher flew down next to her. Laney noticed that he had an old leather pouch slung over one shoulder with a bundle of thin branches sticking out of the top. "What are you doing here anyway?"

He pointed at some trees at the bottom of the hill. "Cutting birch stems over there near the Mencladden Stone." He stopped, as if the rest was a secret.

Laney folded her arms. Why did he have to act so mysterious? Well, she wasn't going to ask what the birch stems were for. He needn't think she was interested.

"Hasn't your dad told you about the rings?" Fletcher added, frowning. "He could have at least warned you about them, even if he doesn't want to join his tribe."

"Of course he told me!" Laney bristled. "Why do you care what my dad does?"

"I don't. You just don't know much yet, that's all. You've only been Awake a few days. Are you sure you'll be all right getting back to Skellmore? You won't get lost or anything?"

To her annoyance she realised her wings had vanished and she was in jeans and a T-shirt again. She flushed. "I don't need any help, so stop bugging me!" She ran off along the riverbank.

It took her nearly two hours to walk the distance that had taken only a few minutes to fly. By the time she reached Skellmore she was hot and tired. The sun was high and the pavements were baking in the summer heat. As she made her way up Oldwing Rise to her house, a knot of worry grew in her stomach. She glanced over the churchyard wall at the broken fence by the pond. She couldn't shake the feeling that the dark figure in her dream was still lurking somewhere.

"Laney!" Claudia hissed at her from behind a tree.

"Why are you hiding?" Laney glanced round. If anyone living on Oldwing Rise looked out of their upstairs windows they'd wonder what was going on.

"Don't go back home yet," said Claudia. "Some

of the faerie Elders are in your house. They waited till your stepmum went out with your little brother and your dad came back from work, and then they went to talk to him."

"How do you know?" said Laney.

"They wanted my mum to go with them because she's the Greytail Elder, but she wouldn't. They're going on and on about the prophecy and she thinks it's all rubbish. She says they've gone to check your date of birth to see if you were born on the night of a red moon."

"Oh. I did tell them when I was born already. Who's in there?"

"Stingwood and Gwen, and that new Mist woman. And some more Elders have come over from Rannerton and Pyton."

Just then the front door burst open and Mr Rivers appeared, red-faced. "And let that be an end to the questions!" he snapped. "The fifteenth of July." He shook the piece of paper in his hand.

A stream of faerie Elders, strangely ordinary-looking in their human clothes, came down the front path. Laney sank back out of view. She thought after she'd been tested that the Elders were going to leave her alone.

Mr Stingwood raised his dark-mahogany walking stick. "You'd be wise not to take that tone—"

Mr Rivers interrupted him by slamming the

door shut.

"That's told them," said Claudia, and she stared at Laney for a moment. "They must be pretty freaked out to come here in daylight. We never usually get together in the village in case people notice."

Laney glanced over at the broken fence in the churchyard again. She had to get a grip. It had just been a dream. She'd had nightmares before.

"What is it?" said Claudia, following her gaze.

"Nothing really."

A little dog came running down the churchyard path followed by a breathless Mrs Mottle, who stopped to watch the trail of people walking away down Oldwing Rise.

"She's one of the reasons we don't get together in daylight," said Claudia darkly. "She spots everything."

CHAPTER 14

Mr Rivers was quiet when Laney got home. His bad mood simmered on for the rest of the day and Laney went to her room straight after tea to avoid it.

She slept badly that night. She dreamed that she was sitting up in bed and looking through the window that she'd left open to keep the room cool. Something was moving. A black shape slid along Oldwing Rise, keeping close to the ground. It paused next to each tree, bush and fence, as if it was searching for something. It passed the house three doors down and Laney was afraid that if it came any closer it would look up at her window and see her...

But the black shape carried on to the end of the lane, and in her dream Laney climbed out of the window and flew after it. It slowed down when it came to the narrow stream outside the village and began to slide along the bank. It was bent right over, almost as if it was sniffing the water. A long dark hood hung down over what Laney knew must be its head.

A creeping coldness spread slowly through her. She shuddered. This icy numbness – she'd felt it before. It was as if her whole body was freezing from the inside.

The dark figure stopped moving along the stream. It stretched out an arm and plunged it into the water. At once, inky-black stains swirled outwards as the water was poisoned by its touch. Laney held back a gasp, sickened by the damage being done to the stream. The black figure pulled an object out of the water and straightened up to its full height. The thing it held was round, about the size of a dinner plate, and it shone in the moonlight.

Holding it high, the dark figure laughed.

Laney woke with a start and sat up in bed. She still felt icy cold. The dream had been so real that for a moment she wasn't sure whether she was asleep or awake.

Moonlight glinted on her open window. Slowly, she peered out at the road. It was completely empty. She shivered. This nightmare wasn't exactly the same as the one before, but it was the same dark figure and this time he had found what he was searching for. All her instincts told her that was a really bad thing.

She closed the window and sat back in bed, hugging her knees. She needed to talk to someone about this. But who? She couldn't tell Kim, because Kim knew nothing about the faerie world. She certainly couldn't tell her dad – he was cross enough already. Claudia might listen, but then again she might treat the whole thing like a joke.

She could ask Gwen. Surely Gwen would know what to do. She checked her clock, which said nearly half past ten. Maybe Gwen would still be awake. She swung herself out of bed, closed her eyes and concentrated on changing into faerie form. She managed it almost straight away this time. Maybe the practice earlier had helped.

Folding her wings into her back, she climbed on to the windowsill and looked over the empty road. The breeze lifted her hair and her heart beat a little faster. Almost as though they had a will of their own, her wings spread out and she let go of the ledge, swooping over the front path.

She flew over the lane and had nearly reached the corner when she heard a snuffling noise. She stopped short and hid in the lower branches of a horse chestnut tree. A fox looked up at her then carried on running, nose to the ground.

Laney breathed out slowly. Daring herself not to be frightened, she flew over the hedge into the churchyard and landed on the gravel path that circled the church. It seemed safer here, away from the houses with all their dark windows where anyone might be watching. She couldn't bring herself to fly above the gravestones though; that was too creepy. She would just walk across to the gate on the other side.

The church soared above her, its spire pointing at the full moon and its pale stones bleached by the moonlight. After the churchyard she would cut across Beacon Way and then over to Gwen's house in Gnarlwood Lane. She would be there in a couple of minutes.

She ran her hand along the church wall and her wings sagged. The night air felt heavy. Putting one hand on the wall to steady herself, she peered round the corner of the church building.

She thought the churchyard was empty until she caught sight of the dark shape hunched over the pond. For a second she wondered if she was still inside her nightmare, but the pitted stone beneath her fingers felt rough and real. As she watched, the dark shape flitted and then crawled, like a giant fly. A bunch of flowers lying on a nearby grave wilted and crumpled as it passed.

Laney's breath stuck in her throat. Coldness crept through her just as it had in her dream. An icy feeling seeped into her chest. She backed away, trembling. Her foot crunched on the gravel path and the noise seemed deafening. She had to get out of here before the coldness took over and she lost the power to move.

Panicking, she flew straight up the side of the church building and over the crest of the roof next to the spire. She landed on the rooftop and folded in her wings. She lay there, with the hard roof tiles digging into her skin and her heart thumping.

Very slowly, she made herself look back down at the graveyard. The dark shape was still there. It stopped for a moment and twisted its long hood. Maybe now it was searching for her.

She had to get off this roof and find Gwen.

The black shape flitted on until it reached the gravel path. Trying not to lose her grip on the roof tiles, Laney sat up and went to unfurl her wings. But they'd gone. Her whole faerie form had gone and she was sitting on the sloping church roof in her pyjamas. It was a long way down with no wings.

She screwed her eyes shut, begging over and over for her faerie form to reappear. At the third attempt, she tried to imagine the river and remember the flow of water against her wings. She felt the change happen, but she still felt weak. Hopefully she would have enough strength to get away.

She slid gingerly down to the edge of the roof, spread out her wings and swooped away over the churchyard. She flew on, hoping the thing didn't come back round the corner, but not daring to look behind.

She reached Gnarlwood Lane without really knowing how she'd got there. A small figure, edged with sparkle, swooped over the other end of the road. A front door opened.

"Sara Thornbeam! Get back in here. It's way past your bedtime."

The sparkling figure flew down and disappeared inside.

The Thornbeam house had an almost bushy appearance. Long branches covered in tiny leaves and dotted with red and white berries stuck out in all directions. Laney turned aside and flew over the gigantic trumpet-like flowers that made up Gwen's roof, but this time there was no coloured smoke wafting from the petals. Trying to calm herself down, she landed in the front garden and knocked softly on the door.

She was scared for a moment that Gwen would be asleep and might not answer. But then the door opened and Gwen surveyed her. She was wearing a straw hat with a ribbon and had a pale-green shawl wrapped around her shoulders. Laney thought she looked as if she was going on a picnic.

"You're shaking, Laney," she said. "What's happened?" She led Laney inside.

Moonlight poured through the glass roof of the plant house, making it as bright as daytime. Gwen sat down and listened intently to Laney's description of the dark shape. Then she shook her head. "I can hardly believe that such a thing was roaming Skellmore. Did you say the flowers withered as it passed? They weren't faded and dry already?"

"They looked fine at first and then they turned completely brown in a few seconds," said Laney.

Gwen's mouth tightened and the lines on her face deepened. "And you say you've dreamed about this *thing* before, ever since you Awakened?"

"Yes. I thought it was just a nightmare until the churchyard fence got broken in exactly the same place as it did in my dream." Laney pulled at her pyjama sleeves. Talking about the dark shape had brought back the terror and made her faerie form vanish again.

"A dream," Gwen muttered. "I wonder..." Drawing her shawl tighter, she got up from the bench and went over to the corner where plant containers were stacked next to the whitewashed wall. She rinsed the dust from a large bowl and then filled it with water before returning to Laney.

"Take this, my dear." She gave Laney the bowl. "Now, touch the water very lightly with your fingertip. As you're from the Mist tribe, you may be able to cast what you've seen on to the surface of the water."

Laney rested the bowl on her knees and touched the water with one finger. "What am I supposed to do?"

"Just stay very still for a moment."

Laney froze with her finger on the water. She dreaded seeing the dark shape in the reflection. But nothing happened.

Gwen sighed. "Never mind, my dear. I've only

seen it done successfully once. Seeing the image would have helped me to be completely certain about what you saw. But you are very new. It was too much to expect really."

Laney put the bowl down. "Do you know what it was?"

"I believe it was a Shadow faerie." Gwen spoke slowly, as if it was hard to let the words go. "The flowers you saw withering are the strongest clue. Only a Shadow can destroy living things that fast."

Laney swallowed. *A Shadow faerie.*

"If you've been dreaming about it," Gwen continued, "then something has connected you to the Shadow."

Laney shivered. "I don't know why."

Gwen poured the bowl of water on to some marigolds, who bowed their thanks. "What about this thing you think it's searching for? Do you know what it could be?"

"Not really, just that it was looking by the pond."

Gwen searched her face for a moment before getting up. "I must speak to the other Elders about what you've told me." With a gentle wave of her hand and a flare of light she changed into faerie form and hovered in the air. Laney gazed up at her, unused to Gwen being taller than her.

"I'll escort you back home," said Gwen. "Then

you must stay inside till tomorrow morning. I'm sure this thing won't dare roam around Skellmore in daylight. Come now, I will give you something to help you feel better before you go."

She flew to the kitchen and poured Laney a glass of something minty green and sparkling from the fridge. "It's Thorn elixir. Try it."

Laney sipped it and it tasted like sweet summer berries mixed with the shimmer of faerie magic. Her heartbeat started to calm down for the first time since she'd left the churchyard.

"Gwen?" she said. "What *is* a Shadow faerie?"

Gwen flew down and landed. Her eyes clouded over, as if she was picturing something from a very long time ago. "Shadow faeries are outlawed because they're not part of the normal faerie tribes. No faerie Awakens as a Shadow; they choose to become one and they do it because they desire more magic. That makes them immensely powerful."

Laney drank some more elixir. "What do they do to get more magic?"

Gwen hesitated. "When a faerie dies all that's left behind is dust, faerie dust. That's what we all become in the end."

Laney nodded.

"Some faeries are so desperate for power that they'll use that dust to make their own magic. It's a very strong spell and it fills them with power. That's when they become a Shadow faerie."

"They'll actually take someone who's died and use them…" Laney tailed off, sickened.

"Yes, and that makes them very dangerous, which is why you should keep as far away from them as possible," said Gwen. "It's a long, long time since we've had a Shadow in Skellmore. I saw one once, but that would have been before you were born." Her tone changed. "Now, let's get you home. Looking at those dark circles under your eyes, I think you ought to get some sleep."

It took Laney a few minutes to change into faerie form. She yawned, struggling to focus. Then they left Gnarlwood Lane and flew across the park together and up Oldwing Rise. Laney gazed all around her, but Skellmore slept peacefully under the full moon. There was no sign of the dark, hooded figure.

"I have something for you." Gwen opened her palm and a bunch of white flowers sprouted in her hand. They had a sweet scent. "Lay these lilies on your bedside table and they'll help you sleep. Don't forget to close the window after I'm gone."

"Thank you!" Laney watched her go, then flew inside and shut the window.

Wanting to keep the lilies alive, she used a glass of water as a vase and stood the flowers in it. Then she lay down in bed and closed her eyes. As she fell asleep she thought she heard the lilies whispering to each other in the dark.

CHAPTER
15

The dark shape leaned right over her, its long hood hiding its face. It reached out a gloved hand…

"Laney, wake up!"

Laney yelled and scrambled into the corner of the bed to get away from that hand, that hood, that burning hate…

"Calm down, it's only daylight!" joked Kim, pulling back the curtains. "I know it's the summer holidays but I don't want you lying in bed all day. It's ten o'clock already."

Laney stared round. There was no black shape. It had just been Kim. She must have been dreaming about that thing again – the thing Gwen had told her was a Shadow faerie.

"Are you all right?" Kim came over and sat down on the bed next to her.

Laney forced her face into a smile. "I'm fine. You just made me jump. I must have been dreaming."

Kim laughed. "I thought maybe you were. You were muttering on about your shadow and how you had to find something. It must have been an exciting dream." She leaned forwards suddenly. "Are you feeling OK? Your eyes are – they look a little red."

"Too much sleep, maybe." Laney blinked and looked away. Kim shouldn't be able to see any change in her eyes, and they were golden, not red.

Kim got up. "I'm taking Toby into town. He needs

some new shoes. Your dad and Simon have gone out. Tea's at seven o'clock. Don't miss it."

"I won't."

Laney got dressed and decided to go to The Cattery, where Claudia lived. She wanted to tell her about last night. Maybe Claudia would know a bit more about Shadow faeries – Gwen hadn't really gone into a lot of detail.

Gusts of wind beat against her as she turned the corner into Beacon Way. She glanced over at the church. Today its walls were as dark and grey as the clouds overhead. Last night she'd been up on the roof, hiding from that horrible dark figure.

She almost wished she hadn't found out what it was. The thought of someone using a faerie's dust – the body they'd left behind after they'd died – to give themselves power, made her stomach lurch. She walked on, imagining that a dark figure might leap out from behind every lamppost.

The Cattery was quiet. A ginger cat sat at the entrance to the street as if it was guarding the way. As Laney skirted past, it turned to watch her with big green eyes. Three faerie houses stood among the human ones. One was a small bungalow covered with sharp brown spines, which growled as she went past. Next door was a grey stone tower, with eyes that blinked from its dark slit windows.

The last one, Claudia's house, was made from

leopard print. The words above the door read: *Do not provoke the beast within*. As Laney approached, the house let out a terrifying roar that made her stagger backwards. She sidled up again, trying to get close enough to stroke the furry wall, when a long leopard-like tail swished down from the roof and knocked her over.

The door opened and Tom Lionhart loped down the path. "Hey!" He slapped her on the back. "Here's the Late Awakening Water Wonder! Burst any pipes lately?"

"Not really." Laney flushed – she could do without Tom's jokes right now.

"Leave her alone, Tom," said Claudia from behind him.

"Sure! I don't want to start a rain shower." Tom peered at the sky in mock fear. Then he climbed into his tiger-like car and roared away.

"Let's go somewhere more private," said Claudia. "I want to talk to you."

"Me too," said Laney. "Something happened last night…"

Claudia shot her a warning look. "Tell me in a minute."

A small black cat ran along behind them as they made their way down the main road. The wind grew stronger and the branches of the oak tree in the park thrashed wildly. Laney caught sight of a bunch of little sprites huddled in the crook of one of the branches. Then she heard a snatch of high, wordless singing. She'd forgotten that Claudia had told her there was a faerie ring in the park. She could see it now, a ring of darker grass in the middle.

A football rolled right through the circle and a little boy ran to fetch it. Laney dashed forwards to stop him but Claudia pulled her back. "Don't worry, he'll be fine. The rings don't affect humans."

The boy ran through the circle of dark grass and out the other side.

Laney and Claudia carried on past the swings. Nearby, three little girls were practising their handstands. As she watched them, Laney realised that they were all faerie children. Did the faerie kids in the village always stick together and play separately from the human kids? Maybe it had always been like this and she'd never known before because she hadn't Awakened.

Sara Thornbeam stopped her handstands and stared at Laney.

Laney stared back, remembering how Sara's brother, Fletcher, had stopped her straying stupidly close to a faerie ring yesterday.

"Who'd want to be a Mist faerie? Water is so boring!" said Sara.

"Shh!" her friend said. "We shouldn't talk about it

out here, remember? And if Jessie hears you, you'll get a soaking!"

"Let's go somewhere where flappy ears can't listen in." Claudia glared at Sara.

They crossed the High Street. The road was busy and everyone seemed to be walking twice as fast as normal. The gigantic green eyes on the wall stared at Laney as she followed Claudia into the Lionhart Pet Shop. Trying not to look at them, she stepped inside and caught her breath. She hadn't come in here since Awakening and now she could feel the strong faerie enchantment in the air. She stopped by a small hutch with five white mice inside.

"Going on the wheel…the whee-l," one mouse sang as he spun round.

"Look! New faerie girl!" said another.

"Claudia! I can hear them!" whispered Laney.

"It's because there's so much Greytail magic floating round in here. It means that all faeries can hear the animals, even if they're not a Greytail themselves," said Claudia. "It only works while you're inside the shop though."

Claudia's dad looked up from behind the counter and his gaze lingered on Laney. "Hello, girls. Don't eat all the biscuits," was all he said.

"No, Dad, we won't!" Claudia went to a small kitchen at the back of the shop with a sink and kettle. She took a tin of biscuits from the cupboard, opened it and offered them to Laney.

"So what did you want to talk about? And why do we have to be private?" said Laney, taking a chocolate biscuit.

Claudia shut the door to the kitchen. "I want to know what happened to you last night. Gwen came to our house early this morning and told my mum and dad that you'd seen a Shadow faerie. They were all really freaked out."

Laney's stomach felt hollow. "Gwen told them herself?"

"Yeah, she's organising a big meeting about it. So what did you really see?"

"There was a dark shape crawling around in the churchyard." Laney flushed, aware of how weird it sounded. "And I had to get away before it saw me. Then I went to Gwen's and told her about it. She said it might be a Shadow faerie."

Claudia raised her eyebrows as she bit into a ginger biscuit. "I used to be terrified by tales of Shadow faeries when I was little. Then I realised that they were in lots of stories, but I'd never seen one. So I figured they were completely made up."

"Gwen said she saw one, years ago," said Laney quietly.

"Really?" Claudia's eyebrows flew up a second time. "I guess she knows what she's talking about then. Anyway, there hasn't been a Faerie Meet for ages. Shame it's only adults allowed. Maybe we should sneak up there and listen to what they say."

The sound of voices came from outside the kitchen and the door swung open.

"There you are, Laney." Gwen stood in the doorway in a raincoat and a waterproof hat. Claudia's dad looked over her shoulder. "I need you to come to Skellmore Edge. It's very important."

"You mean, right now?" Laney thought of the Edge, which towered over the village, with its flat stony top. It would be the most windswept place they could go on a day like this.

"Yes. Please come straight away. I need you to tell everyone at the Faerie Meet about what you saw last night."

CHAPTER 16

"I'm not being tested again, am I?" asked Laney.

"It isn't a test, my dear," said Gwen. "All you have to do is tell them what you saw. Now I must go. I need to talk to the other Elders." She went down the rabbit food aisle and Mr Lionhart opened the door for her.

Laney and Claudia followed them outside. The day had turned darker. Black clouds had swollen into a great rolling mass on the western horizon. Lightning flashed as they stepped out on to the High Street and its jagged shape stayed imprinted on Laney's mind long after it had vanished.

"I'll meet you on top of the Edge," called Gwen as she hurried away. "Don't be too long; the others won't want to be kept waiting."

A drum roll of thunder followed her words and the gigantic cat eyes on the wall blinked rapidly.

"Are you OK, Laney?" Claudia's eyes were wide. "I'm seriously glad it's not me having to face all those adults. Everyone from all the villages will be there – Thorns, Greytails and Mist faeries. There'll be loads of them."

Laney swallowed. "I feel a bit sick."

"Here, try a custard cream. That always works for me." Claudia thrust one into her hand.

Jessie crossed the street and stopped in front of them. "If there's a way to turn back into a human, you'd better do it right now, Laney, because you're

going to be *so* busted!" She swept back her curly
hair and walked off.

"Really great to see you too, Jessie!" Claudia
called after her.

"She's right. They're going to ask me loads of
questions and I don't know anything," said Laney.

"Don't stress out. Just tell them what you saw,"
said Claudia. "I'll come with you and wait just
below the top. I want to hear what they say."

A black cat slipped out of the pet shop to join
them. "Are you coming with us, Dizzy?" said
Claudia.

The cat swished its tail before streaking across
the road and out of sight.

"They don't like it when all the tribes get worked
up like this," said Claudia. "They're very sensitive to
faerie magic."

Laney's stomach lurched. The custard cream
hadn't helped at all. "I'd better go."

They walked together up Beacon Way until they
reached the end of the village where the rows of
houses became hedgerows and grass. Climbing
over a stile, they followed the footpath across the
fields. The rocky face of Skellmore Edge loomed
over them.

"It would be quicker to fly up." Laney looked
behind her to check if there was anyone else nearby.
"No one's looking."

"We can't. They'll use the Mist tribe to bring down the fog and hide the whole Meet from human eyes. It's really thick stuff. We'll never manage to fly through it."

Within a few minutes Laney began to understand what she meant. A white haze rolled over the top of the Edge. At first she thought it was no different from any other fog, but it thickened fast. The ridge of the hill disappeared from view almost at once and a few minutes later she could barely see her own feet. "I can't see where I'm going. How are we supposed to find our way through this?"

"I guess we just keep on climbing," said Claudia.

"The Edge is a huge place though. We could end up in completely the wrong part." Laney tripped over a hawthorn bush and fell over. "Ow! This is stupid!"

A dark shape appeared close to them, making them jump. "I can take you up to the top," said Fletcher. "I know the way really well."

"I thought only adults were allowed at the Faerie Meet," said Laney.

"They won't know I'm there. I'll stay out of sight," said Fletcher.

"What if your dad spots you?" said Claudia.

"He won't. I'm a Thorn – good at camouflage, remember? Anyway, I want to know what's going on. The adults never tell us anything." He glanced sideways at Laney.

She knew he was wondering about what she'd seen and what she was going to tell the adults, but she didn't feel like explaining it right now.

As they scrambled through the bushes and brambles just below the peak, Laney could see that Fletcher wasn't the only one who'd decided to listen in. There were several faces she recognised from the school bus, hiding behind rocks or shrubs. They were mostly kids in the years above her at school who lived in Pyton or Gillforth.

Soon the earth footpath turned to stone. "You're nearly there now. Just keep going," said Fletcher in a low voice.

"Good luck," Claudia whispered to her.

Laney climbed the last few metres alone on to the uneven rock of Skellmore Edge. As she reached the top she broke through the white haze into open air. The fog formed a ring around the edge of the flat hilltop, leaving the middle completely clear. There was a patch of blue sky overhead, but the storm clouds still hung in the west.

A grey-haired man stood on the cliff, blowing hard into his cupped hands. As he opened his fingers and spread them wide, clouds of vapour went billowing away to add to the fog around the slope. Further along, more faeries were doing the same, building up the fog bank to hide the meeting from human eyes. Laney knew they must be from the Mist tribe and she wondered if she'd be able to do the same thing one day.

A crowd of people parted to let her through and whispers followed her as she walked across the hilltop. Her foot caught on a rough piece of rock and she staggered, but recovered her balance. She glanced back, realising she'd fallen over a gouge in the rock shaped like a pair of giant footprints. Shuddering, she wondered whether those really were boot marks set into the stone.

"Laney!" Gwen called her over. She was standing at the centre of a small group of people and Laney noticed silver markings on the backs of their hands. These must be the Elders. Fletcher's dad and Claudia's mum were there. The cold-eyed Miss Reed stood with them too. Her lips curled mockingly when she saw Laney.

Everyone was in their human form, but an unmistakable shimmer in the air gave away the presence of magic.

"Is this the girl?" shouted someone from the back.

"Yes, this is the girl." Mr Stingwood loomed up behind Laney, his face like stone. "Mrs Whitefern has spoken about what you told her. Now we want to hear it in your own words. What is this thing you think you saw and why is it so important that we all have to meet up – at great risk of being discovered by the humans." He cast a stern look at Gwen.

"Just tell them what you described to me last night," said Gwen. "Take your time and remember as much as you can."

A great hush fell over the hilltop and dozens of pairs of gold-ringed eyes fixed on Laney.

CHAPTER
17

"Well, I—" began Laney.

"Speak up and tell the whole Faerie Meet," interrupted Mr Stingwood, waving his walking stick towards the throng of people.

Laney looked at them all and almost lost her nerve. Gwen gave her an encouraging smile. "Well, I was walking through the churchyard last night, and suddenly everything felt scary. That's when I saw a dark sort of *thing* near one of the gravestones." She shifted from one foot to the other.

Mrs Lionhart frowned. "And did you go any closer?"

"No, I didn't want it to see me."

Gwen cleared her throat. "Laney came to tell me what she'd seen and when she told me how a bunch of flowers on a grave wilted as this figure passed by, I remembered that this was a true sign of a Shadow faerie. A Shadow is the only thing I know of that can destroy living things so swiftly."

"What did this dark thing do?" Mr Thornbeam asked Laney, his serious grey eyes reminding her of Fletcher.

"It moved around, like it was looking for something. It was searching at the edge of the pond," said Laney. She could hear voices growing louder at the back of the crowd.

"Is there anything else you can tell us about it?" said Mrs Lionhart. "Any more details of what it looked like?"

"It was sort of hard to see. It was a black figure and I thought it had a hood..." She trailed off. How could she make them understand? The feeling of terror had been so strong; she couldn't have looked any closer.

A ripple of laughter broke out on one side of the hilltop.

"Does she expect us to believe this was a Shadow faerie, just because it had a hood?" said a grey-haired man with a thin moustache like cat whiskers. "And how *can* it be a Shadow? No one's seen one for years. Are we supposed to believe that something as bad as that – something that can turn you to dust in seconds – is suddenly here in Skellmore?" He glared at Laney. "Or is this just a girl's wild imagination?"

Laney flushed. She hadn't even told them that she'd dreamed about the dark figure before seeing it in the churchyard, although Gwen knew. If they found that out they would really think she was crazy.

"Why should we trust a girl who hasn't Awoken till the age of twelve?" added Miss Reed. "And whose father refuses to behave like one of us?"

Laney's hands balled into fists. They'd better leave her dad out of this.

"We can't ignore the possibility that it *was* a

Shadow," said Gwen sharply. "I know we can't be certain yet, but if we do nothing then we'll be ignoring the danger."

Tom Lionhart stepped forwards. "How do we know that you Thorns aren't trying to distract us from something else? Like something that's happening in the deep parts of Hobbin Forest. The cats say there's a part of the woods where they can't go, some kind of secret area where no one knows what's going on. What is it you're doing in there?"

"Silence!" Stingwood shook with pent-up rage. "*You* are under age and you're not even supposed to be here. How dare you try to spy on us using dumb animals?"

Tom opened his mouth to reply but his mum pushed him aside easily, despite her small size. "Believe me when I say that we Greytails will not be taking any insults from the Thorns!" she growled. "What *is* your tribe doing in the forest that's so secret?"

Gwen looked surprised. "I don't know of any Thorn project in the forest. Do you, Peter?"

"It's none of the Greytails' business what we do in our forest." Stingwood held Mrs Lionhart's stare. Gwen frowned and the crowd's muttering grew louder.

"Listen!" Gwen held up one hand and spoke to

the mass of faeries. They fell silent immediately. "We won't get anywhere by arguing with each other. Fighting among ourselves will play right into the Shadow's hands. This is a dangerous time."

"We already know that," replied a thin woman with waist-length hair. "We saw the Wolf Moon three nights ago, just after we found out that our Mist Elder, Arthur Puddlewick, had died. It was so sudden – he was very well a few days before."

A rumble broke from the crowd at the mention of Puddlewick's death.

"The Wolf Moon is at the centre of all of this," said Stingwood. "And that is why this girl, who Awoke on that exact night, is not to be trusted. She turned the river that monstrous colour. Who knows what else she's done?"

Mrs Lionhart drew herself up to her full height, which was still half the size of Stingwood. "*We* do not indulge in ridiculous superstitions." Her eyes flicked to Laney. "And maybe there *is* something… unusual about this girl. But maybe the red moon is a sign that a whole tribe is dangerous – and I bet that tribe is the Thorns!"

"You're a fool!" someone yelled from the back.

"You should stop spending time getting cosy with the humans and learn proper faerie ways!" snarled Stingwood. "*She's* the one that Awoke under the red moon. I say that if the signs show something bad is coming, then that bad thing is her." He jabbed his finger at Laney.

Laney's face flamed and she made herself speak. "I haven't done anything. You made me do that test and you didn't find anything wrong."

"But, Peter," said Miss Reed, ignoring Laney's outburst, "you saw me do the test on her. There was virtually no Mist power there at all. I don't think we can even let her into our tribe with so little ability."

"I've heard more about what she's done since then. Her friends have told me how close she came to exposing us with her antics at school. The child that told me is a Mist faerie too." Stingwood glowered at her. "So pipe down and remember that *you* are not an Elder!"

Miss Reed flinched. She began to protest but her voice was drowned out by the shouts of other faeries. In the distance, the dark clouds thickened and thunder rumbled.

Laney's mind worked furiously. Who had told on her? Nobody who was a real friend. A Mist faerie, he'd said, so it had to be Jessie. She'd probably lied and said they were friends.

"Faeries, this is a warning." Gwen spoke over the noise of the crowd as she pointed at the thunder clouds. "Shadow faeries used the cover of storms to work their dark magic in the old days."

But Laney noticed that the faeries had stopped

listening. They were shifting on the hilltop, gathering into groups and one by one they changed into their faerie forms. A breeze lifted with the movement of dozens of wings.

A scuffle broke out in one corner. A Mist faerie blasted ice across the hilltop. One Greytail summoned a group of crows that swooped over to attack.

Gwen changed to faerie form in a blaze of light and flew over the hilltop, stopping the ice arrows from hitting their target.

Stingwood raised his walking stick and a myriad of prickly vines sprouted from gaps in the rock and snaked across the hill.

"Greytails, defend yourselves!" shouted the man with the moustache, before a vine curled round his ankles and pulled him over.

Laney looked on in horror, jumping when someone grabbed her shoulder. "Laney, move!" said Fletcher. "You have to get out of here."

Loose stones slid under Laney's feet as she fled, nearly tripping over the giant rock footprints for a second time. She ran after Fletcher into the band of fog that surrounded the hilltop. Then she blinked, trying to see where he'd gone. Icy droplets from the fog condensed on her hair.

Fletcher seized her hand and pulled her sideways. Branches moved and Claudia climbed out of her hiding place, twigs catching at her jeans. Then they half slipped and half ran down the hillside together.

The yelling went on above them. Laney heard Stingwood shouting but she couldn't hear what he was saying. A blast of heavy rain hit them, nearly knocking them over.

"Watch out!" yelled Fletcher, and Laney turned to see a volley of spiky cacti shooting down the hillside.

"Was that meant to hit us?" gasped Laney.

"I'm not staying to find out!" Claudia accelerated, bounding easily over the rough ground.

They raced to the bottom and scrambled over a stone wall, taking shelter on the other side.

Laney pressed her back against the stones and tried to stop her legs shaking. "Do they always fight like that?"

"They've completely lost it!" said Claudia. "Those Thorns…"

"It's the Greytails – always making fun of what we believe in!" snapped Fletcher.

"We don't believe the Wolf Moon is such a big deal, that's all," said Claudia.

"The Mists, Blazes and Kestrels believe in it too." Fletcher glared at her. "You're too busy pretending you're human to see what's important."

"OK, truce, guys," said Laney. "I've really had

enough of this right now." She could hear her own pulse thumping. She rested her head on her knees for a second.

A group of figures flew overhead, their wings moving like a whisper. Sections of fog began to curl away into the sky.

"It sounds as if the Elders have stopped the fighting," said Fletcher. "I guess they won't be calling another Meet for a while after this disaster. Here." He pulled a bottle of water from his pocket and offered it to Laney.

"Thanks." She took it, but as her hand closed round the plastic, the liquid inside began to bubble. Claudia's eyebrows rose. Laney handed the water bottle back unopened.

"They didn't believe me about the Shadow faerie," she said miserably. "Most of them thought I was lying."

"They were pretty harsh," said Claudia. "It was like they'd already made up their minds."

"I believe you," said Fletcher abruptly.

"Really?" Laney studied his face, but he looked serious.

"Yeah, I mean, if that's what you saw in the churchyard then that's what was there," he said. "Gwen says it sounds like a Shadow faerie and I trust her too." He got up and shoved his hands in his pockets.

Laney looked at him gratefully. "I wish I'd been able to describe it better, but I didn't want to get any closer to it last night." She shivered. "I didn't know a Shadow faerie could turn you to dust in seconds, like that man said."

"That's what they do in the stories," said Claudia. "This red energy comes out of their fingertips and... *kabam!* You're lying dead on the floor. I seriously thought they were only stories though."

"Red energy?" said Laney.

"Like lightning," said Fletcher.

"Did you see the big footprints set into the stone at the top?" said Claudia. "The story goes that they were made by a Shadow faerie in the middle of some huge battle."

"Yeah, I saw them." Laney didn't add that she'd nearly fallen over them.

"You can't really miss them," said Fletcher.

Laney didn't answer. She couldn't stop thinking about her dream from last night. It had seemed so real. The more she thought about it, the more she was sure that she'd been seeing the same dark figure in her dreams ever since she'd Awakened. If Claudia and Fletcher heard that, they'd think she was making up the whole thing.

She scrambled up and headed for the footpath that led back to the main road. "If the grown-ups won't look for the Shadow faerie then I'm going to.

Then they'll have to believe me."

"Are you mad?" Claudia ran to catch up with her. "You should avoid Shadow faeries, not go looking for them. What are you going to do if you find it?"

"It's not often I agree with a Greytail, but she's dead right," said Fletcher. "You've no idea how dangerous it would be." He clicked his fingers and a low-hanging tree branch moved aside to let them past.

"But I think it's hunting for something." Laney scraped back the wisps of hair falling over her face. "And we don't even know what that is. And the tribes don't want to believe any of it."

The thunder clouds marched across from the west, covering the sun.

"But seriously, Laney," said Claudia as they turned on to the main road that led back to Skellmore. "How are you going to find it anyway? I mean, nobody else has even got a glimpse of it except you. What makes you think it's going to keep appearing for you, as if you're something special?" She broke off, staring at Laney.

"Just leave it now, Claudia," said Fletcher.

"Hold on! Maybe that's it." Claudia's eyes widened and the gold rings inside them became huge. "Maybe it's only appearing to Laney for a reason. Maybe it's something about *her*."

"What do you mean – because of that red moon

on the night I Awakened?" said Laney.

"You're a Greytail. You don't believe in that," Fletcher told Claudia.

"I know…" Claudia carried on staring. "It's weird though, isn't it?"

Laney swallowed. "Look – I'll see you later, OK?" And she ran off down the road. She was used to Jessie being mean to her, but she'd just begun to think that she and Claudia were friends. Now it seemed that Claudia thought she was a freak too.

CHAPTER
18

A car sped past as Laney reached the first houses on Beacon Way. Then a tractor chugged up the road, pulling out to avoid the parked cars. Its engine was so loud that she didn't hear Craig Mottle cycling up behind her.

"Hey, Lane the Pain!" he taunted. "Are you looking for some more losers to hang out with?"

Laney slowed down, wishing she had some kind of useful faerie power that could make annoying boys explode. "Shut up, Craig. You're just embarrassing yourself."

"Oh yeah? You're the embarrassing one, you—"

"Craig! She said shut up!" Claudia stood behind him, arms folded.

Craig eyed her. He was clearly wondering where she'd appeared from so suddenly, but the thought was taking a while to reach his mouth. "Where did you—"

Laney rolled her eyes and walked off leaving him in mid-sentence.

"Lane the Pain!" he yelled behind them.

"It's sad that he thinks that's a good insult just because it rhymes," sighed Claudia.

Laney stared down at the path. Claudia's comment about her was still going round in her head. *Maybe it's something about her… It's weird though, isn't it?*

"Once, when Craig *really* annoyed me," said

Claudia, "I got the cats to sing outside his window all night. They did 'Baa Baa Black Sheep'. It's one of their favourites but they don't really sing it in tune."

Laney couldn't help grinning.

"What I said before – I didn't mean it like that," said Claudia. "I didn't mean that *you* were weird."

"What did you mean then?"

"I meant last week you were just another human and now you're in the middle of this huge thing that's causing trouble between the tribes. I've never seen them as jumpy as this before."

Footsteps made Laney look round, but this time it wasn't Craig. "I think you're right, Laney," said Fletcher. "I've been thinking about it. If there's a Shadow faerie around we have to track it down, even if it's dangerous. Once we've got some evidence, we can make the other Elders believe in what you saw."

"Did you finally catch up with me then?" Claudia brushed a leaf off her jeans. "Thorns aren't really built for speed, are they?"

"I had to hide. The Elders were trying to catch all the kids that shouldn't have been up there. Look, I want to help you," he told Laney. "I don't think you should search for this thing by yourself."

Laney's cheeks reddened. "You don't have to. I don't want to get you into trouble. But I know I have to find out what this Shadow faerie is doing because…" She hesitated, but the secret was pressing down on her and she hated the heavy feeling inside that it gave her. "Listen, I'll tell you something if you promise not to tell anyone else."

Claudia's eyebrows shot upwards. "I promise. What is it?"

Laney looked at Fletcher. "I won't tell," he said.

"I saw the Shadow faerie before I even went through the churchyard," she said. "I saw it in a dream last night. That's why I'm sure it's looking for something. In the dream it picked up a round thing, but I couldn't tell what it was. It seemed pretty happy about finding it, in a horrible sort of way." She stopped, afraid to look at their expressions.

"You dreamed about the Shadow faerie?" said Claudia. "Are you sure it was the same faerie?"

"Yes, I'm sure. Gwen said maybe something had connected me to it." Laney faltered, noticing how grim Fletcher's face looked.

"That's not good," he began.

"No, it's great!" said Claudia. "We can do a dreamwalk. That's when you go back into your dream and see what's really happening. It's something no other tribe can do except the Greytails."

"Bad idea," said Fletcher. "Dreamwalks are dangerous."

"What do *you* know?" snapped Claudia. She turned to Laney. "I can take you back into the dream and you can sort of relive it. It should be easy as you only dreamed it last night – the dream should be fresh in your mind."

Laney tried to smile. She wasn't sure she wanted to go back inside that dream. It had been pretty scary the first time. "Will that really help?"

"Of course," said Claudia impatiently. "You'll be able to see the dream again and I'll be there too. Between us we can work out what the Shadow faerie's looking for and what it's planning to do."

Fletcher folded his broad arms. "Don't expect me to join in with it. You're mucking around with serious magic."

"Fine by me, twig boy," said Claudia. "We don't need you anyway."

"That's good then!" Fletcher walked off, hands in pockets.

"Fletcher?" Laney called after him, but he was already halfway down the road.

"Forget him," said Claudia. "Thorns are always a bit like that. Stuck in their ways – they hate doing anything unless they're in charge of it. They're a strange kind of tribe really."

"OK, tell me what we have to do," said Laney, wondering if Greytails were just as strange in their own way. Claudia seemed a bit too excited about the whole dreamwalk thing.

Laney left the house by the front door that night as

her dad and Kim had gone to bed early. Flying out of the window was exciting, but it was probably safer this way. She glanced back at the dappled watery light playing across their cottage, and then she crept along to The Cattery with her pillow tucked under her arm. Claudia had told her to bring an object that had been close by when she dreamed of the Shadow faerie. Hopefully the pillow would be all right – she'd been pretty close to it after all.

The houses of The Cattery growled sleepily. Claudia appeared through a gap in the hedge at the bottom of her garden. A small black cat skulked at her heels. "Did you get away without anyone seeing you?"

"Yeah, it was easy." Laney held the pillow firmly.

"There's one more thing we need before we start," said Claudia, hurrying off down the road.

Laney raised her eyebrows. "What's that?"

"Fletcher."

"But he said he wouldn't be a part of it, remember? And you told him we didn't need him!"

"I know, but I forgot that we'd need someone to stay outside the dream – just in case. And I don't want to ask another Greytail to do it."

"Have you ever done a dreamwalk before?"

"Yes." Claudia paused, before adding, "But it was on a cat. They have dreams too, you know, mostly about chasing things."

Laney didn't find that very comforting. Being out here in the dark when the Shadow faerie might be around was already giving her the shivers. "Maybe we should find another way to work out what the Shadow's doing. I don't want it to go wrong."

"But this is the best way. Your dream could have an important clue. It's just a shame it's not a full moon any more, because our powers are at their strongest then." Claudia glanced up at the moon, which looked as if a creature had taken a small bite from it.

They found Fletcher crouched up a tree in a field behind Gnarlwood Lane. He spread his grey wings and leaped to the ground. "How did you know I was here?"

"I'm a Greytail. I can track things," said Claudia impatiently.

"You were out looking for the Shadow faerie, weren't you?" said Laney.

Fletcher folded his wings behind him. "Yes I was. My mum and dad say there isn't one, but sometimes I think they don't want to admit what's really going on. I thought I'd wait here and listen. There have been strange whisperings from the trees lately."

Laney couldn't help gawping at him. How did trees whisper? Thorn magic was a bit strange. Claudia nudged her.

Laney sighed. She knew what she was supposed

to do. "We need someone to be with us while we do the dreamwalk. We were hoping you'd do it?"

"*She* didn't want my help before," said Fletcher, turning his gaze on Claudia.

"It would be safer with someone else there," said Laney. "Please?"

Fletcher paused before straightening his shoulders. "All right then. I doubt it will work anyway."

Claudia sniffed, but didn't say anything.

"Thanks." Laney was just glad to avoid another argument.

"Why don't we go to Hobbin Forest? No one will interrupt us in there," said Fletcher.

"What if those hobgobbit things come along?" said Laney. "And Tom said there was something dodgy going on in the forest – something that some of the Thorns are doing."

"Oh, the Thorns are always up to something," said Claudia. Then she saw Fletcher's face. "I didn't mean that in a bad way! Maybe those trees over there would be all right. They'd give us enough cover." She jerked her head towards a small group of trees on the other side of the field.

"Fine, let's just start," said Laney, beginning to feel nervous.

They crossed the field, climbed the fence and entered a small copse where the dark tree branches closed over their heads. Claudia stopped by a fallen tree trunk.

"There's no one around," said Fletcher. "Except…" He frowned and put his ear up against a tree trunk.

Laney looked at Claudia. "What's he doing?"

"It's a weird thing that Thorns do," said Claudia. "Don't ask me – I've got no idea!"

"It's not weird," said Fletcher. "We can find things out from the trees…like messages."

"Like you're using a tree phone!" said Claudia. "Actually, can you find out the football results for me?"

Laney managed not to giggle.

"Yeah, yeah, very funny." Fletcher thrust his hands in his pockets. "Anyway, listening to trees is a lot more sensible than doing a dreamwalk."

"It'll work. You'll see." Claudia changed into faerie form, flexing her wings. "OK, are you ready? You need to be in faerie form."

Laney handed her pillow to Fletcher, who put it down on the fallen tree trunk and sat on it. She closed her eyes and concentrated hard, managing to change into faerie form almost straight away. She stretched her wings.

"Hold up your hands like this." Claudia held her hands up, palms forwards, and Laney placed her hands against them. "Now close your eyes and try and remember the start of the dream."

Laney shut her eyes. She'd been in her room. It was night-time and she'd been looking through the window. Was that how the dream had started or what had really happened? Somehow it all seemed the same.

Her stomach dropped. She felt like she was falling and falling and she would never stop.

CHAPTER
19

And suddenly she was there, sitting up in her bed.

Cool night air flowed into the sweltering room through the open window. Down the lane, something was moving…

"What are you looking at?" hissed Claudia. "Is it down there – the Shadow?"

Laney stifled a scream. "Where did you come from?"

"I'm supposed to be here," said Claudia. "I'm walking your dream with you. This *is* the right dream, isn't it?"

"This is the right dream." Laney leaned closer to the open window, watching the dark shape gliding down the lane, close to the ground. When it was right outside her house, it stopped and its black hood slowly swivelled to the side.

"What if it sees us?" Laney covered her mouth with her hand.

"If it didn't see you the first time then it won't now," said Claudia. "The dream can't change. It's already happened." But she ducked down out of sight all the same.

The dark figure moved on and the girls breathed again.

"That thing is majorly freaky." Claudia shivered. "OK, what did you do next?"

"I followed it and it went down to the stream at the end of the road." Laney checked over her shoulders, but from the draught of air she already knew her wings would be there. Dream wings, she thought.

Claudia opened her wings too. "You go first – you know what's going to happen. I'll follow you."

Laney swooped from the open window and flew along the road just as she had dreamed the night before. She landed at the end of the lane and scanned the dark fields in front of her. Everything felt even more real this time. She could hear a night bird calling and smell the muddiness of the stream. The Shadow faerie would be down there, ready to pull that round thing from the water. She felt like she was taking part in a play, acting out something when all the scenes and lines were already fixed...

She gasped.

"What's wrong?" Claudia landed behind her.

The dark figure was halfway up the slope and moving back towards them.

"It's not supposed to be there. It's supposed to be standing by the stream like it did last time," said Laney. "Quick – hide!"

The girls ran to the nearest fence and knelt down behind it.

"What exactly did it do in the dream?" whispered Claudia.

"It stayed by the stream and it pulled something

out of the water. Then the dream ended." Laney crouched as low as she could.

The figure stopped, its dark hood clearly outlined against the moonlit sky. Then it glided away down the street.

"Are you sure this is a dream?" said Laney. "Look, the moon isn't the same either. It's a three-quarter moon and it should be a full one."

The huge moon hung in the sky, with a bite taken out of it.

Claudia gripped her arm. "Never mind the moon. Where's the Shadow faerie gone?"

Laney ran out from behind the fence to look down the street, and suddenly the world spun. When it stopped she and Claudia weren't next to the houses any more. They were standing in a field outside Skellmore, with the wide river glittering in front of them and the wooden bridge stretching across it.

"We've moved," hissed Claudia.

Laney pulled Claudia down behind a bush. "The Shadow's over there." She pointed at the dark figure, now bending down by the river just metres away. With a jolt, she realised that a feeling of deep cold was stealing through her. It made her arms feel heavy and slowed her heartbeat. Something about the dreams or the Shadow always brought this same feeling, as if her body was turning to ice.

"This is all wrong," Claudia whispered. "The dream isn't supposed to change. We have to stop this and wake up. To end the dreamwalk we just—"

"Wait." Laney's breath stuck in her icy throat. There was something different about the figure of the Shadow faerie – something about the way it was standing that made her sure it had found what it wanted. This was the reason they'd come here tonight.

The Shadow plunged one arm into the water and, just as before, inky-black stains swirled outwards as the water was poisoned by its touch. Then, with slow triumph, it pulled out an object that was round and beautiful. A swirling pattern ran around the edge of the object, and in the centre was a sheet of crystal that turned the reflected glow of the moon into a thousand lights.

"A mirror," whispered Laney, and as she stared into the mirror's heart she saw a terrible picture. In the reflection, the river water rose up and covered the village. Every road became a grey torrent and water lapped at front doors and downstairs windows. No grass could be seen in the park, except for the perilous circle of the faerie ring. People stood at their upstairs windows, cut off by the rising flood. Kim and Toby called out to her, and they sounded frightened.

"No! You can't do that!" Laney croaked. She

sprang from her hiding place and tried to run, but her frozen legs wouldn't work. She had to help them before it was too late.

The Shadow's head began to turn…

Claudia grabbed Laney's hands and held them palm to palm with hers. "Laney, don't move! We have to get back before it sees us."

Laney caught the fear in Claudia's voice and held her hands still. If this was just a dream, then it would soon be over…it would soon be over… But the Shadow lifted the mirror even higher and she couldn't take her eyes away from the picture inside.

"Wake up!"

The ground felt hard underneath her back. Fletcher's face loomed over her. "Wake up!"

"All right, I'm awake!" Laney sat up, her head spinning. She was still under the canopy of the trees where they'd started. The riverbank and the dark figure had vanished, and that awful iciness that filled her body had gone too. She gave a shudder of relief.

Fletcher shook Claudia, who was lying on the ground, her eyes still closed.

Claudia twitched and opened her eyes. "That was *not* a dream."

"What was it then – a trip to the moon? I've been shaking both of you for five minutes," Fletcher said angrily. His fringe was sticking up and his jeans were covered in leaves.

"The dream went kind of wrong. It wasn't the same as before," said Laney. "We didn't stay in the right place. We should have stayed by the little stream."

"It was *seriously* wrong," said Claudia. "In dreamwalks, the dream is *always* the same as the first time. *That* was more like a spell and it was freakin' scary! If that thing had seen us…"

"Maybe you did it wrong," said Fletcher.

"No!" Claudia glared. "I'm sure it wasn't a dreamwalk at all. Maybe it's because we're doing it under these stupid trees. This place is too full of Thorn magic. Maybe that turned the dream into a spell instead of what it was supposed to be."

"It was your idea to come here. And don't ever try that again," Fletcher said flatly. "I'm not staying to watch next time. I wasn't sure I could get you back."

"Don't worry, Thorn boy. I won't be doing that again," said Claudia. "Not even for a cat's nine lives."

"But at least now we know what the Shadow's looking for." Laney got up shakily. "We saw what he's been trying to find. It was that mirror – I remember it now – the one in that Tale of the First Faeries that Gwen showed me. He held it right up in the air."

"What do you mean? The Shadow faerie wasn't

holding anything," said Claudia.

"Yes it was! That great round mirror," said Laney. "The moonlight shone off it really brightly – you must have seen it."

"If it's in the Tale of the First Faeries, then it has to be the Crystal Mirror," said Fletcher.

"There was nothing there," said Claudia.

"If it was the Mist Myrical it would make sense that Laney could see it and you couldn't," said Fletcher. "Because she's from the Mist tribe."

"I remember Gwen saying something about Myricals," said Laney.

"They're the things that hold the essence of each tribe's power," said Fletcher. "That's why there are five of them – one for each tribe. There's the Wildwood Arrow – that's our Thorn Myrical. Then there's the White Wolf Statue that belongs to the Greytails, the Crystal Mirror that belongs to the Mists, the Sparkstone of the Blaze tribe and the Kestrels' Vial of the Four Winds. My dad says they were all hidden away years ago."

"What did this mirror look like?" demanded Claudia.

"It was round with a pattern along the edge, but instead of glass it had a surface that reflected lots and lots of ways all at once – like a diamond. When the Shadow faerie pulled it out of the river he held it up really high." Laney shivered.

"It sounds like the Crystal Mirror," said Fletcher. "The legends say it holds the key to your tribe's power."

Laney thought of the bright mirror with its thousands of reflections and her skin tingled. She could imagine how amazing it would be to have the key to all water magic in her hands.

There was a scuffling noise a little distance away. "Let's go," said Fletcher. "The trees are worried."

He changed to faerie form, spread his wings and soared up between the branches.

Claudia rolled her eyes. "The trees are worried! Maybe they've got caterpillars eating their leaves."

Laney unfolded her wings and flew up into the night sky. Clutched by a terrible thought, she veered left over the fields towards the river.

"Laney, wait," called Claudia.

"I've got to look at the river," Laney called back. She heard the beating of her friends' wings as they hurried to keep up with her, but she didn't slow down. What if the picture in the mirror was true? What if something terrible had already happened to Skellmore?

Finding the glittering curve of the river, she flew over and landed on the bridge. The others flew down behind her.

The river looked just the same as always. No dark figure. No flood.

"Why are you smiling?" said Claudia.

"It wasn't true," she said. "In the mirror, I saw the river bursting and covering Skellmore. There was water everywhere and it felt like it was really happening – the whole village was really in danger. But it wasn't true."

"It could be what the Shadow *wants* to do," said Fletcher grimly. "If he's looking for the Mist Myrical, then he must want to use it for something. Myricals are supposed to hold a lot of power."

"You mean he could use this mirror against us?" said Laney.

Claudia and Fletcher exchanged looks. "The Myricals have been lost for years. I don't really know what they do," said Claudia. "There's a tale about how all the Myricals were lost because a Shadow faerie tried to take them. I thought it was just a scary story, but then I never believed in Shadows until today…"

Laney stared at the village lights twinkling beyond the dark water and she thought of Kim and Toby at home in bed. "The Shadow's hunting for the mirror. That's what he wants. And we know he's out there, but there are a lot of people who have no idea what's coming."

CHAPTER
20

"Where are you going?" yelled Claudia as Laney lifted into the air. "You can't keep rushing off!"

"I'm going to tell Gwen about the Crystal Mirror," Laney called back, swooping over the river. "She's the only one who believed me when I saw the Shadow faerie."

"We believed you too," grumbled Claudia.

"Then come with me," said Laney.

Fletcher took off, joining her in the air. "Gwen will know what to do."

"You *hope* she will," said Claudia.

They flew down to the ground at the end of the High Street, changed to human form and ran across to Gnarlwood Lane. The village was eerily quiet, although Laney noticed more cats than usual sitting on walls and skulking under hedges.

The trumpet-shaped flowers that formed Gwen's roof glowed faintly, but the rest of her house looked dark.

"Fletcher! Thank goodness." Mrs Thornbeam, Fletcher's mum, appeared out of the darkness. Her mouth tightened when she saw Laney and Claudia. "We found out you weren't in your room and we didn't know where you'd gone. It's not safe out here."

"Mum, you know I'm fine. I have my Thorn power." Fletcher looked embarrassed. A cloud of pink and white sprites flew over to settle on his shoulders and he brushed them off quickly.

Laney ran up Gwen's front path and knocked on the door. Gwen would know what to do. Gwen would look at her with those wise eyes and understand what she'd seen in the mirror.

"Gwen's not there," said Mrs Thornbeam.

Laney's heart sank. "Where's she gone? Will she be back soon?"

Mrs Thornbeam was silent.

"Mum! When will she be back?" said Fletcher.

Mrs Thornbeam eyed Laney doubtfully. "She's travelled north to talk to more faerie Elders and I don't know when she'll be back." She shook her head. "After all that's happened today, you three go flying about like nothing's the matter."

"But we know what's going on—" started Claudia.

"No, you don't. You don't understand at all or you wouldn't be doing this. A Thorn, a Greytail and a Mist together? For goodness' sake!" She raked a hand through her hair. "You can't be friends. Not any more. And if the other faeries see you together like this they could throw you out of your home and banish your families from Skellmore."

Fletcher stared at her. "You've always let me talk to Mists and Greytails. I know them from school."

"Talk to them, yes, but not be close friends. Times are changing. Who knows how long the tribes will even carry on talking to each other?" She turned away. "I'm going to tell your dad that you're back."

Laney, Claudia and Fletcher looked at each other.

"Look," said Laney. "I know things are bad but we have to do something about the mirror – try to find it ourselves. We can't wait. If the Shadow gets it first he could do anything…" She thought of the image of the flood in the mirror and how it had drowned Skellmore in a torrent of grey water.

"How do we know he hasn't found it already?" said Claudia.

"I think if he had, the village would be flooded right now." Laney bit her lip. "Will you help me?"

Fletcher nodded. "I'm in."

Claudia shuddered. "I hate water. If the mirror's in the river, then you'll have to be the one to get it, Laney."

"Meet me by the bridge in the morning and we'll start searching," said Laney.

As Claudia and Fletcher left, Laney closed her eyes to wish herself into faerie form, then stopped. Somehow it felt too dangerous to fly back to Oldwing Rise, as if someone might be watching the skies.

As she ran round the corner into her road, Jessie stepped out from behind a lamppost. The orange light glinted on her sleek wings.

"Don't think you can join our tribe, Laney Rivers," she whispered fiercely. "After the joke you made of yourself at the Faerie Meet today, no one else in our tribe wants you either!"

Laney glared back. "I don't want to join your stupid Mist gang anyway."

"Too busy running around with a lying Greytail, are you?" spat Jessie. "There's something wrong with you. Just look at what happened on the day you Awakened. We had a red moon – the worst sign in the faerie world – and our Mist Elder, Arthur Puddlewick, died. What does that tell you?" She spread her wings. "You'd better watch it because I'm going to prove you can't be a Mist faerie." And she swept into the air and flew away.

Laney lay awake in bed that night, afraid to close her eyes. She'd left her pillow behind at the place where they'd done the dreamwalk and the rolled-up jumper beneath her head wasn't very comfortable. She didn't want to dream. She didn't want to see the Shadow faerie, watch that long hood turning slowly towards any sound…

But she was exhausted and sleep took over.

She sat up. The pale moonlight trickled over her bedcovers. A tiny breeze came through the open window. That settled it. She knew she'd shut that window. She'd checked it three times. Now it was magically open again. This was definitely a dream.

Trying to shake off the shivery feeling, she drew closer to the window and looked outside. She knew it would be there – that dark shape gliding up the lane. She leaned back against the wall, keeping as far away from the window as possible. This didn't have to be the same as last time. She just had to stay here in her room until she woke up. Then she wouldn't have to see the Shadow searching for the mirror. She wouldn't have to feel afraid.

She folded her arms, wishing she had the guts to reach out into the night and pull the window closed.

Minutes went past. Had the Shadow gone by? Did it know she was up here? She shook herself. How could it know? This was just a dream.

Unable to stop herself, she peeked out of the window.

A tide of grey water was sweeping along the road, seeping under cars, flowing through hedges and lapping at doorsteps. The flood was coming. Behind her in the darkness, she heard Toby crying.

She woke up.

Laney couldn't sleep for the rest of the night. At daybreak she went downstairs, stuffed her rucksack full of food and left a note for Kim. She glanced at her dad's work schedule, which lay open on the kitchen table. It said that he and Simon were working somewhere in town, installing a new bath and shower for a customer. She was glad that her dad would be out of the way.

She left the house quietly and walked to the river. Putting down her rucksack, she got out some food and ate breakfast sitting on the bridge. She thought about the dream from the night before and how dangerous the flood had seemed. She stopped when she noticed a whirlpool forming in the middle of the flowing river, sucking in any leaves and branches flowing past. She took a deep breath to calm herself and the whirlpool disappeared. Perhaps she shouldn't think about the dreams, not when she was so close to water anyway.

Claudia and Fletcher appeared on the footpath leading down to the bridge.

"So where do we look for this mirror?" said Claudia, climbing on to the bridge. "I mean, if it's been hidden for this long, it's not exactly going to be easy to find, is it?"

"I was going to find the place on the bank where the Shadow stood in my dream, the place where he lifted out the mirror," said Laney. "I think I know where it is." She hid her rucksack behind a bush and led them along the riverbank. The rough path turned into bare mud that had cracked in the summer heat.

"Here!" said Claudia. "I remember the shape of the bushes and the bend in the other side of the river."

Laney stood right on the edge and stared down into the clear water. "I don't see anything." She knelt down, ignoring the nettles, and plunged one arm in the river. "I thought I'd know when I found it. It's supposed to be full of Mist power so I should be able to feel it, shouldn't I?"

"Of course you'd feel it," said Claudia impatiently. "But seriously, why would it be here? You said the first dream showed the Shadow faerie pulling it from the stream at the end of your road. Then we see him take it from the river. He doesn't know where the mirror is either."

"Except that he's looking underwater each time," said Fletcher.

Laney pushed her hair out of her eyes. "But there are so many watery places to look. There's the river and the stream. There's a pond in the churchyard and a small one in the Mottles' back garden, and there are some pools in Hobbin Forest too."

"We need a map of the area," said Fletcher. "Then we can check them all one by one."

Claudia yawned. "Isn't there a quicker way?"

"I doubt it." Fletcher eyed Claudia with amusement. "And if that flood really happens, all the Greytails will get soaked. So let's get on with it."

"We might get soaked soon anyway. Look at that!" Laney pointed into the distance. "Those are the blackest storm clouds I've ever seen."

CHAPTER
21

Claudia and Fletcher exchanged looks.

"What's the matter?" said Laney.

"In the old stories, when a Shadow faerie was doing something bad they always raised a thunderstorm to hide their spells," said Claudia.

The black clouds rolled forwards and turned the fields below dark.

"Then we have to work faster than the Shadow." Laney closed her eyes and changed into her faerie form. "You two keep an eye out for humans while I check each pond and stream. I can fly right through the water. It'll be quicker."

Laney dived into the river. She glided quickly through the water, checking every bank and reed bed for signs of the Crystal Mirror. By the time she had checked several miles of river and the smaller stream, the storm clouds hung right over their heads and little black storm flies crawled across their skin.

"Do you think the Shadow knows we're looking for the mirror too?" said Claudia. "This isn't normal – these storm clouds—"

"There's someone over there – hide!" said Laney.

They ducked behind some bushes as a figure came into view. Jessie came down the footpath and stared into the stream at the exact same place where Laney had just been searching. She walked up and down for a while, before heading towards the footbridge. The others climbed stiffly out of their hiding place.

"What's she up to?" said Claudia. "She looks pretty suspicious."

"I bet she's looking for me," said Laney. "She told me last night that she was going to make sure I didn't join the Mist tribe. So much for Mist team spirit." She remembered something else that Jessie had said. "And she was blaming me for the death of the Mist Elder on the night I Awakened. I don't know why it was supposed to be my fault."

"You mean Arthur Puddlewick?" said Fletcher. "I thought he died of old age."

"Strange that it should all happen on the same night though," said Claudia.

"Oh, don't go on about that again!" said Laney.

"No, I just mean…why *did* it all happen on the same night? It's weird." Claudia stretched in a graceful, cat-like movement.

"It's a pity he died actually," said Fletcher. "If anyone would know where to find all the ponds and streams, it would be—"

"The Mist Elder," finished Laney.

"Exactly!" said Fletcher. "My dad keeps a record of all the trees in this area, from each small copse up to the big forest. So why wouldn't the Mist Elder do the same with the rivers and pools?"

"If he left any information behind, it would make

searching a lot quicker." Claudia's eyes gleamed. "Shall we go and look?"

"No!" said Fletcher. "No way! If the other Elders catch us sneaking round his house they'll go mad."

"I think it's a great idea," said Laney.

"He lived in Gillforth, didn't he?" said Claudia. "Do you think we can fly there without being seen?"

"I think we should try." Laney checked all around for signs of Jessie and then launched herself into the air.

Fletcher groaned. "If we have to do something stupid, let's at least choose the safest way to get there." And he led them away from Skellmore and over the river. They flew over dozens of fields of sheep and several farm buildings before the village of Gillforth came into view. Laney's wings began to get tired.

"Talk about taking the long way round," grumbled Claudia as they landed behind a hedgerow and changed back into human form.

A tortoiseshell cat appeared from the undergrowth and watched them curiously.

"We need to know if Arthur Puddlewick's house is empty," said Claudia. "Could you look for us, please?" The cat flicked its tail and ran off.

Laney cast a look back at the storm clouds. This had better be worth it, otherwise they were just giving the Shadow extra time to work his spells and find the mirror himself.

The cat reappeared after a few minutes and uttered several long mews.

"It's empty," Claudia told the others. "The downstairs has been locked up but there's an upstairs window they forgot to close."

They followed the tortoiseshell cat into the village. There weren't many people around, only a man mowing a front lawn and some little kids playing on bikes down the road. Trying not to look suspicious, they walked up a gravel drive to a small house with a rectangular pond and a beautiful fountain in the front garden.

Laney looked at the house, expecting to see some sign of Mist power, but the bricks were bare and ordinary.

Fletcher saw her looking. "The power dies with the owner of the house, but it did look great when he was alive."

"Come on." Claudia hurried down the side alley. "Before someone thinks we're burglars or something."

The open window was at the back. Claudia changed to faerie form, flew up to the window and slipped smoothly through the small gap. After a few moments she opened the back door from inside.

Laney's heart jolted as she went in. Saucepans lay upside down on the kitchen floor. The cupboards were open. A trail of earth from a house plant was scattered over the worktop.

"It's like this upstairs too," said Claudia.

"Maybe burglars have been here," said Laney, walking into the sitting room and gazing at the books lying upended on the carpet.

"Or maybe someone else had the same idea as us," said Fletcher. "Maybe they were looking for information too."

Laney scanned the room, taking in the pictures of calm rivers and stormy seas on the walls and the mess on the floor below. "It's horrible that someone's already been here. It's bad enough thinking that we're going through a dead man's stuff."

"It'll be worse if that someone is the Shadow and it comes back again," said Claudia. "Let's get a move on."

Laney looked in the cupboards. If there was a map or a list of rivers and ponds, maybe it would be stored away safely. Finding nothing, she moved on to the bookcases. Then she checked everywhere else.

Fletcher turned over the sofa cushions. "Maybe this wasn't such a good idea. There's nothing here."

"Can't you use your Mist senses, Laney?" said Claudia. "Maybe there's a Mist-type clue around here."

"Maybe he didn't write anything down," said

Fletcher. "Maybe we're looking for something that doesn't exist."

"Stop being so gloomy and let her sense something," snapped Claudia.

Laney looked round the room. Did she even have any Mist senses? Maybe she wasn't powerful enough for that. She chewed her lip, trying to concentrate.

"Are you feeling anything Mist-like?" asked Claudia.

Laney sighed. "Everything here feels Mist-like, so how am I supposed to find something important among all the other Mist-type things? It's impossible to—" She broke off. There was one way to go straight to the heart of Mist magic.

She ran to the kitchen, found a washing-up bowl and filled it with water.

"What are you doing?" said Claudia.

"Trying something out." Laney hurried back in with the bowl of water. "Watch out."

Claudia dived round the back of the sofa while Fletcher hid behind the door. Closing her eyes, Laney willed the water to spread far and wide as she flung the bowl into the air. The bowl bumped down on to the carpet. When she opened her eyes again, everything in the room was wet. Water dripped from the ceiling and sparkled on every inch of the windows. The water had scattered just as she'd commanded. Now she had to work out if anything was different.

Claudia jumped up from behind the sofa, her long black hair dripping. "Laney! I'm soaked!"

"Sorry." Laney scanned the room. Nothing seemed to have changed...except something about the picture next to the bookcase was different. The painted sea looked wilder and the thrashing waves reached up higher. She unhooked it from the wall, turned it over and ran a finger round the edge of the frame. A tiny corner of white showed at one side. She took hold of it carefully and pulled, and a small piece of folded paper slipped out.

She put down the picture and unfolded the paper. It looked old and the lines on it were drawn in black ink. There was a long curved mark across the centre and she knew at once that this was a map and the long line must be the river.

A jangling noise came from outside and a key turned in the front door. Laney, Claudia and Fletcher raced through the kitchen, out of the back door and along the side alley. They could hear voices at the front door.

"What makes you so sure they came over here?" said Miss Reed in her usual cold voice.

"I followed them out of Skellmore. They were heading in this direction but then I lost them," replied Jessie.

Laney's hand gripped the wall. So Jessie had carried on spying on them.

"What is this mess?" Miss Reed's voice rose. "The tribe will be furious that Arthur's home has been treated this way. We must prove that this was the Rivers girl. Then it will be impossible for her to get Mist training. I wish we could get her whole family out of Skellmore. Her father is a disgrace, the way he ignores our tribe."

"She's made friends with a Greytail. I wish that was enough to get rid of her!" said Jessie.

"Now that she's invented this story of seeing a Shadow faerie, it should make things a little easier," Miss Reed said. Their voices faded as the front door shut behind them.

Claudia's gold-ringed eyes blazed. "Those sneaky little—"

"Don't," begged Laney. "There's no point."

"Why aren't you angry?" whispered Claudia furiously. "They're such mean, stupid, lying Mists!"

"Not so loud," muttered Fletcher.

"It's not exactly news that Jessie doesn't like me, is it?" Laney waved the map in front of Claudia's eyes. "Stuff Miss Reed! I can't let the Shadow start a flood in Skellmore. If he gets the Crystal Mirror, no one will be safe."

CHAPTER
22

The storm clouds hung over Skellmore for the rest of the afternoon. Thunder rumbled now and then but no rain came.

Laney, Fletcher and Claudia fell into a pattern of searching. Fletcher read the map and found the next pool or stream, and then Laney would scour the water for the mirror. Each time, Claudia used her Greytail abilities to track the living things around them and check that they weren't being watched.

Laney felt increasingly drained by changing from human to faerie form and back again. The image of the mirror with its glistening sheet of crystal grew larger in her mind, and with it grew the picture of the flood that she'd seen inside the mirror. Was the Shadow searching too, under the cover of the storm clouds? And if the storm started, would the flood start as well?

They came to a small pool in Hobbin Forest just as the sun began to set. Laney heard a faint singing and knew at once that there was a faerie ring not far away. The high song rippled through the air, drawing them in. Laney looked through the trees and thought she could see the ring, half hidden by dead leaves. Maybe she should just take a look.

She stepped towards it, but Claudia stopped her. "You'd better be quick," she said. "There are hobgobbits about half a mile away. If they catch our scent they'll attack. They're creatures of the forest and they hate anyone else being here."

"After this pool, there are only two more in the forest to check." Fletcher peered at the map in the fading light. "Then we'll have to search the ponds in Skellmore or go to Faymere Lake on the other side of the woods."

"All right, here I go." Laney touched the water with her hands. This way she'd found she could get a feel for how deep it went. Then she folded her wings behind her and dived in. More than ever she was amazed at how right she felt flying through the water and how she didn't need to breathe. She searched the pool for any sign of the Crystal Mirror, especially under the stones at the bottom. She was sure she would get a hint of its power, even if it was partly buried. No, it wasn't here.

But something was different.

Through the sway of the water she could hear a faint wordless singing. It was the sound that came from inside the faerie ring. She could hear it even underwater. Ignore it – it's dangerous, she told herself and flew up towards the surface.

"I don't think there's anything here," she told the others. "Let me just have one more look."

"OK, but then we need to get to the other pools," said Fletcher. "It'll be harder to search once the sun goes down. More dangerous too."

Laney knew what he meant. She'd been thinking

it too – it might be easier for the Shadow to work his spells once the sun went down.

"You know, this Shadow faerie must have belonged to one of our tribes once," said Claudia. "Isn't that a seriously horrible thought?"

"He could be from the Blaze or Kestrel tribes, not from one of ours." Fletcher looked up from the map.

"I suppose," said Claudia.

Laney hesitated. "You don't think… You don't think this Shadow faerie has a human form too, do you?"

Claudia looked horrified. "Maybe they do. Then how would we know who they are?"

"We probably wouldn't know until they transformed into their Shadow shape," said Fletcher grimly.

"Then they could be anyone. We could walk past them without even knowing," said Laney.

"Don't think about it." Fletcher returned to the map. "Let's just get this Crystal Mirror."

Laney dived into the pool and searched the water again.

"No sign of it?" asked Claudia as Laney climbed out.

"Nothing." Laney frowned. It was harder to hear the music of the faerie ring when Claudia kept talking, and she wanted to hear it better.

Claudia tensed. "The hobgobbits know we're here. They're coming."

"I'll get rid of them. You guys get up into the trees. They can't reach you there." Fletcher grabbed a fallen branch from the ground.

"OK, Mr Thorn Hero!" Claudia flew up and perched on a branch.

Laney spread her wings to do the same, but she was too slow. Fallen leaves flew up into the air and a squat shape rushed right at her. She tried to dodge, but the growling thing knocked her off her feet.

"Get off her!" shouted Fletcher, hitting it with his branch.

More leaves flew and a whole gang of hobgobbits lurched towards them.

"Take that!" yelled Claudia, pelting them furiously with sticks from the safety of her branch.

"Laney! Here!" Fletcher threw his branch to her and grabbed another for himself. "Just smack them as hard as you can. It's the only thing they understand."

Laney struck the nearest one with the stick. She did it softly at first because the creature was small – barely up to her waist – but when it ran at her a second time she hit it harder.

Fletcher clicked his fingers at the nearest trees. They immediately swept their branches down and began to knock the hobgobbits flying.

Laney groped for some Mist magic. Maybe she could help with a burst of water. Why couldn't she find any magic when she needed it? She stumbled backwards and the hobgobbits followed.

"Mind the faerie ring!" yelled Fletcher.

Laney felt the energy of the ring more strongly now. Half hidden beneath the dead leaves, the dark circle filled the air all around with powerful shimmering magic. She edged away, fighting the longing to get closer to it.

Snarling, the hobgobbits charged. There was a blur of pitted brown bodies and flailing branches. Then a high yelp.

Laney gasped. One of the hobgobbits had got too close to the ring.

The creature was frozen in mid-air, its head tilted back and mouth open. The air around the faerie ring throbbed with energy. A spiral whirlwind surged upwards, sending the hobgobbit spinning.

Laney reached out, thinking to save the creature, but the whirlwind sucked it down into the ring and it was gone. The other hobgobbits shuffled away into the undergrowth without a sound.

Fletcher dropped his branch.

Claudia flew down from her tree. "I don't like those things, but that was horrible."

Laney stared at the dark circle of grass. "Can't we help it? Rescue it?"

The others shook their heads. "The rings are a gateway to the Otherworld," said Claudia. "I don't think anything ever comes back."

They were silent for a moment. In the gathering dark, Laney's throat tightened. The loss of the hobgobbit left her feeling empty, as if the hungry darkness of the faerie ring had taken part of her too.

Fletcher unfolded the map again. "The other pools are just over here. Come on." He folded up the paper and trekked off through the trees. Laney went after him, the image of the falling hobgobbit replaying in her head. Claudia followed in silence.

They reached a part of the forest where the trees grew more closely together. As darkness grew, the birds stopped singing. Laney felt a tingle on the back of her neck and told herself not to be silly. There was no need to freak out just because it was getting dark.

"I've found it," said Claudia, springing through the undergrowth and landing by a pool with cat-like grace.

Fletcher checked the map. "There should be two ponds. The second one must be over there." He strode off, calling back. "Yes, it's just here. They're quite close together."

Laney got ready to dive into the first pool. "The water's moving." She tested the gently swirling water with one hand.

"It must lead somewhere," said Claudia. "Maybe there's a stream that feeds into it."

"I don't think so," said Fletcher, looking again at the map.

Laney felt her excitement rising. She dived into the first pool and searched it thoroughly, before returning to the surface disappointed. Another ripple passed her. There was definitely something funny about the water – she felt full of energy, as if they'd only just started the search.

Rushing through the trees, she plunged straight into the second pool and let the water stream over her wings. The water felt great here too, but she still didn't find anything.

"There's nothing here." She flew out and shook water from her hair.

"It's strange that the water's moving," said Claudia.

"It shouldn't be." Fletcher studied the map. "There's nowhere for it to go."

A silver fish swam to the surface of the pool, almost shining in the darkness.

Fletcher bent his head close to the map, trying to see it better. "That's it. We've checked everywhere in the forest, and the river and the stream too. That just leaves the man-made ponds back in Skellmore. And also Faymere Lake, which is huge."

"Is this where we are now?" Laney pointed at the

map. "What's that dotted line?"

"Just a sec – we need some light." Fletcher looked up and whistled.

A cloud of tiny sprites drifted down through the branches and hung over the map and all around Fletcher's head. Their petal-like bodies had a soft glow that lit up the paper.

"That's handy," said Laney drily. "If these are the two pools I've just searched, why would there be a line between them?"

Fletcher grabbed one of the sprites and held it closer to the map. It squeaked indignantly.

"Don't hurt it!" said Laney.

"Don't worry, it's fine," said Fletcher. "You're right, the line stretches from the edge of one pool to the other."

"Maybe Puddlewick's pen slipped when he made the map," said Claudia.

Laney stared at the dotted line, her pulse quickening. "Or maybe it's something else. I'm going back in!" And she dived into the pool.

The water was dark but something luminous and silver flitted past Laney's face – the fish she'd seen before. She caught her breath. There was a whole cloud of them. She began checking the sides of the pool for signs of the mirror and the fish followed her.

The silver shoal hung for a moment next to a

large boulder wedged into the mud. Laney stopped to look and the stone trembled as she touched it. She dug her fingers behind the boulder and pulled and pulled, until finally it shifted to one side.

A gap opened up where the boulder had been. Air bubbles streamed from the newly made hole and beyond there was a place lit by a whitish glow. This must be why there was a dotted line drawn on the map. Between the two pools lay a tunnel, like a tiny underwater world.

CHAPTER 23

Laney decided there was no time to explain her plan to the others. She squeezed through the small hole and flew on into the tunnel. Strange fish in colours from gold to electric blue swam past her and the walls were lined with weird-shaped coral. One fish nibbled her finger before darting away again. This was underwater heaven, except for the icy cold. Maybe it was cold down here because it never got any sunlight.

Carefully, she ran her hands along the tunnel wall, searching for something – a smooth patch or anything that felt different. The mirror *had* to be here. Its Mist power must have made this place special. As she moved on, the tunnel narrowed. Afraid of getting stuck, she twisted back and grazed a wing against the wall. A dot of white light appeared where her wing scraped the tunnel and she reached out to touch it with her fingertips. The light grew underneath her fingers, casting rays of silver through the water.

Laney scratched at the tunnel wall, digging her nails into the mud as she tried to reach the light underneath. The earth came away in clumps, muddying the water as stones broke off and sank to the floor. This must be it! She could see something now. It was a curved edge decorated with a criss-crossing pattern, just the same as the frame of the Crystal Mirror from her dreams.

She took hold of that edge and pulled. For a second nothing happened. Then a mass of soil and rock came away and she was left holding on to a heavy round object. It shone even brighter now that it was free from the wall, and the water around it churned wildly. Laney felt like her blood was churning too. This was the Crystal Mirror. The power coming from it felt awesome and the silver light was almost blinding.

Laney darted away, afraid that the falling earth and churning water might make the ceiling collapse. She pushed the mirror along in front of her as she flew towards the hole at the end of the tunnel. Thrusting the mirror through the narrow gap, she climbed through after it and shot up towards the surface.

"Laney!" Fletcher leaned down to haul her out of the pool. "What have you been *doing*?"

"He's been going mental," said Claudia. "He was trying to persuade me that we should go in to rescue you. Me and muddy water – it was never going to happen."

"I'm fine," gasped Laney. "Look!" She carefully placed the mirror on the bank, before taking Fletcher's hand to get out of the pool. Sitting up on the grass, she tried to shake off the icy feeling that had seeped into her inside the tunnel.

The mirror's silver brilliance faded a little but the

air around it quivered with magic. Laney knelt over it, fascinated by the surface of crystal that glittered like a thousand stars.

"I can't believe you found it," said Claudia. "Where was it?"

"There's a tunnel between the pools – an underwater one," said Laney, leaning closer to try to make out the reflection in the mirror.

"So that's what the dotted line on the map is," said Fletcher. "That makes sense. But we should get moving. Other things could be drawn to the power coming from the mirror."

He bent down to take hold of it but Laney pushed him off. "Wait! Don't you get it? This has all of the power of the Mist tribe inside it."

"I know, it's one of the five Myricals and that's why we have to take it back to the Elders," said Fletcher.

"I wouldn't give it to a Thorn faerie, not unless it was Gwen and she's probably still away," said Claudia. "That Stingwood man is really mean and I don't trust him. Miss Reed looks dodgy too."

"Have you lost your mind? We can't keep it ourselves!" snapped Fletcher. "We have to get it back to Skellmore and give it to *all* the Elders. *They'll* make sure it's safe."

"And what if they don't? What if they fight over it?" said Claudia.

Laney reached out to touch the mirror. She could hear Fletcher and Claudia arguing behind her but their voices sounded muffled, as if someone had turned the volume down. She felt dizzy, and when her hand met the sheet of crystal, a tingling sensation ran up her arm. She felt connected to the power in the mirror, as if she could do anything – bring water out of solid rock or lift up a whole lake if she wanted to.

Now she would show Jessie and Miss Reed. She had the essence of Mist power at her command. They would beg her to join their tribe.

She still felt very cold but she didn't care. She'd found the mirror! She placed her pale, frozen hands on its surface and gave a happy sigh. The breath curling from her mouth was freezing cold too, and it looked strange, like a cloud of thick red fog. She pulled backwards in alarm.

She'd seen fog like this before…and felt this deep cold… She'd been freezing cold every time she'd dreamed about the Shadow and his search for the mirror. She'd felt it during the dreamwalk too.

The weird-looking vapour twisted and turned, spreading outwards rapidly. It crept over the ground and across the still pool. Laney stood up, shuddering as she felt a cold wisp curl around her knees.

"What's happening?" said Fletcher. "Laney, what

did you do? What is this red stuff and why did it come out of you?"

"I don't know!" Laney cried. "It was in my breath."

"Why?" Claudia's voice rose. "What haven't you told us?"

"Nothing, I swear!" said Laney.

The reddish fog climbed to waist height, curling and swirling as if it was alive, and suddenly Laney remembered exactly where she'd seen it before. The night she'd Awakened, the night of the red moon, there had been fog just like this. She had breathed it in and felt so cold, and at the same time she had seen the dark figure...

Laney picked up the heavy frame of the mirror. "We've got to take this far away, somewhere it can't do any harm." She broke off as the fog surrounded the Crystal Mirror, covering its bright surface. Then the mirror gave a pulse of dazzling light and all the fog vanished completely.

Laney caught her breath. The mirror had beaten the fog. It had won.

"It is finished," said a voice full of horrible triumph. "The spell is complete." A dark shape swept over their heads with its huge black wings stretched wide.

The Shadow faerie landed and the trees around it wilted and turned brown within seconds. Leaves withered on the branches before dropping to the ground. The black figure towered over them all and the air reeked of decay.

"No!" whispered Laney.

The Shadow rounded on her and folded its vast wings. A hood hung right over its face, but as its head turned Laney thought she caught a glimpse of its eyes – black eyes full of creeping malice. It stretched out its fingers, pointing at each of them in turn.

Laney found that she couldn't move. She could barely lift her eyes to see that Claudia and Fletcher were motionless too. They were all helpless.

"Your part is over," said the Shadow. "You have brought me the mirror, just as I knew you would."

Laney tried to move her lips to speak, but no sound came out. The Shadow waved his hand and she found her mouth unfrozen. She moistened her lips. "But you were searching for it yourself. I saw you."

"That was my first plan," the Shadow hissed. "I prepared my enchantments, making them so powerful they could not fail to unearth the Myrical. Then just as my spell was perfect, you blundered along and breathed in my spell fog. Stupid girl!" He snapped his fingers and a crowd of tiny ice arrows flew at Laney. She couldn't move to dodge them and they struck her like little knives before falling to the ground.

The Shadow clenched his fist and after a moment he regained his control. "You took the core of my finding spell with you that night and then only you had the power to discover where the Crystal Mirror was hidden, and retrieve it."

Laney's mind flashed back to the orange-red fog near the faerie ring on the night she had Awakened and how cold she had felt after breathing it in. That same feeling – being frozen from the inside – had come back time after time. "It must have been the spell working every time it wanted me to look for the mirror," she muttered.

"Once I realised what you'd done, I knew I had to make you find it for me. It was simple to pretend to hunt for it. It sparked your curiosity – always a useful failing of the ignorant." The Shadow gave a cold laugh.

"You made us think you were hunting for the mirror." Fletcher struggled to speak. "But we were doing what you wanted all the time."

"And there is one more thing you will do for me. Give me the mirror and then I will destroy you with the rest of your village." The Shadow stretched out his hand and the mirror wobbled.

Laney's mind reeled. She tried to hold tight to the Crystal Mirror but her fingers were stiff with cold.

"Laney!" rasped Fletcher. "Don't give it to him—"

"None of you can stop me." The Shadow sounded

amused. "And this is what happens if you try." A bolt of red lightning shot from his gloved fingers. It hit Fletcher in the stomach and he tumbled backwards through the trees.

Panic rose in Laney's chest. In his frozen state Fletcher wouldn't be able to work his wings to save himself. Next to her, she could see Claudia wriggling her fingers to try to break free from the Shadow's spell hold. Her heart thudded as she tried to do the same. She could move her fingers a little but her hands felt strange and heavy. She tried harder and managed to move one arm. Then she stopped, terrified in case the Shadow saw.

"It took you long enough to accomplish the task of finding the mirror," continued the Shadow. "But of course you do come from a second-rate family. Now I shall have what I came for." He moved towards her.

Laney twitched one arm, and then moved her legs. She had done it – she had broken out of the Shadow's spellhold. This was her chance.

With a strength born of panic, she held tight to the Crystal Mirror and launched herself into the sky. Straining her wings, she flew up high, carrying the mirror in both hands. A gust of wind nearly blew her into a tree but Fletcher grabbed her arm and pulled her away.

"Fletcher! You're all right!" yelled Laney.

"Just fly, Laney!" he shouted back.

"He's coming!" screeched Claudia, swooping beside them.

Crack! Red lightning blasted into a tree right next to them. Laney felt the heat of the attack on her wings and back. The tree gave a long creak and toppled over in slow motion.

She sped up, not looking back. *Crack!* Red lightning shot past her legs. Losing her balance, she went spinning sideways. She hit her head against something hard and fell through a net of branches, still gripping the mirror. Branch after branch broke beneath her and finally she crumpled to the ground. The Shadow faerie landed next to her, a spark of red lightning still crackling from his gloved fingers.

He took the Crystal Mirror, which slipped easily from Laney's grasp. For a moment, he leaned over it. His breath left no mist on its crystal surface, which made Laney wonder if he had any breath at all. Then he laughed and opened his great, black wings. The air around him festered like rotting meat. Laney's stomach heaved and dark blotches swam in front of her eyes.

The Shadow held up the mirror and the glistening crystal surface darkened until Laney saw the grey river, rising up and spilling over its banks, filling Skellmore with a tide of water. Kim and Toby stood at the upstairs window of their house, calling out to her…

"Say goodbye to Skellmore, because there won't be anything left of it after tonight." He soared into the air and flew off into the darkness.

CHAPTER 24

Claudia flew down between the branches. "We have to get out of here before he comes back."

Laney staggered to her feet. "He won't come back. He's got the mirror now and he's going to use it to drown Skellmore."

"He's so strong," said Claudia. "We'll never stop him."

"We can at least warn everyone. If we tell the faerie Elders, they can get people out of the village," said Laney.

"Are you sure he doesn't just want you to think he's starting a flood?" said Fletcher. "What if it's another trick? We've already helped him once by finding the Crystal Mirror for him."

Laney's shoulders sagged. "I know. It's all my fault. But I didn't know I was helping him."

"I'm not blaming you." Fletcher took off into the air. "But we have to find out if he's telling the truth. If there's a flood, it'll start with the river."

Laney and Claudia followed him into the air, but Laney's wings felt shaky and she found it hard to keep up with the others. As they left the forest behind, a gigantic fork of lightning burst out of the storm clouds in front of them, pointing straight down at Skellmore. Then the rain started.

At first, there was a scattering of raindrops. Then the shower quickened into a pitiless torrent.

Laney peered through the grey curtain of rain.

The river rolled and churned below them – the wooden bridge was already underwater and only the top of the railing was showing. She remembered her rucksack that she'd left under a bush near the bridge that morning. It had probably been washed away by now.

"The river's already over the top of its banks," yelled Claudia.

"It won't be long until the water reaches Skellmore," said Fletcher. "Once it gets to the top of that footpath then there's nothing to stop it – it'll just run down the hill into the High Street."

"I can't fly for much longer in this rain." Claudia shook the water from her wings.

"Why?" asked Laney.

"I haven't got water wings like you," said Claudia. "Only Mist and Kestrel faeries can fly in heavy rain."

Laney's heart sank. "But I'll need your help to fly people to safety."

Claudia stared. "Are you mad? The Elders will never let you get the humans out like that. You'll expose the whole faerie world!"

"I don't care about your faerie secrets! We need to make sure everyone's safe – that's a lot more important than the faerie world." Laney wheeled round and flew towards Skellmore. At least she knew her dad would be on her side. He would want to get people out quickly, even if the tribes didn't like it.

She landed on the edge of the village, raced down the road and into the churchyard, taking the shortcut for home. As she sprinted up the path, she saw a large group standing by the church entrance. She heard raised voices and several people turned towards her, their gold-ringed eyes easy to spot even through the heavy rain.

"Here she is!" Jessie broke away from the group, pointing at Laney. "It's nothing to do with the rest of the Mist tribe. It's all *her* fault."

"Don't be silly," said Mrs Lionhart. "How can one child be doing all of this?"

Claudia and Fletcher raced through the gate behind Laney.

"A Thorn faerie with a Mist and a Greytail!" Mr Stingwood waved his walking stick at Fletcher. "What is wrong with you, boy? You insult all Thorns by behaving like this. Stick to your own kind!"

Mrs Lionhart glared at him. "Be quiet, Peter! This isn't the time for one of your rants." Her firm manner instantly quietened the group. She turned to Claudia. "Where on earth have you been?"

"Mum, I can't—" Claudia searched for words to explain. "I know I've been gone for ages, but there's an emergency!"

"There's a flood coming," Laney burst out. "And

226

we have to wake people up and get them out of Skellmore."

"See? She knows there's a flood because she's the one who made it!" cried Jessie. "You can't blame the whole Mist tribe for this – it's just her! And she's been trying to do bad things at school too. I saw her down by the bridge today and she must have done something to make the river burst its banks. We all know she Awakened on the night of the red moon."

"But it can't be her," said Miss Reed. "The test showed that her Mist power is tiny."

"Maybe she had someone to help her," growled Stingwood. "Maybe she and her dad did this together. Come here, girl. Explain what you have done."

"I haven't done anything!" Laney's voice rose in desperation. "And my dad's not even here. He's working." She hesitated. None of them believed in the Shadow faerie. She needed a way to make them understand the urgency.

"Never mind all the accusations," said Mrs Lionhart. "Can't you Mist faeries go down to the riverbank and hold back the flood with your powers?"

None of the Mist faeries spoke. Miss Reed flushed with embarrassment.

"They've already tried and failed," said Stingwood

contemptuously. "But we can take *her* down there. Then we'll see what she can do." He jerked his head at Laney. "Girl, I said come here!" He thumped his walking stick on the ground and huge thorns sprouted all the way down the length of it.

Laney felt like backing away, but didn't. "We have to get people out of Skellmore."

There was a flash of lightning and someone knocked Laney over on to the grass next to a gravestone.

"Stop it!" shouted Mrs Lionhart. "This is not the way!"

Still shocked by her fall, Laney pushed her hair from her eyes and looked round the side of the gravestone. Stingwood was tangled up in a tightly knotted vine. He struggled to reach his spiky walking stick, which lay on the ground, and tiny bolts of white lightning began shooting from his fingertips. She pulled herself up to a crouch, still hidden behind the headstone.

"Stay still, Peter, and I'll try to untie you," said Mrs Lionhart. "Who did this to you?"

A bolt of lightning broke through the clouds above, followed by thunder so loud that it echoed round Laney's head. Another smaller flash of lightning came from Stingwood's fingers. Suddenly his hands shook and bolts of electricity shot in all directions. There were shrieks and the faeries scattered.

Laney crawled along the wet grass between the gravestones, hoping that Stingwood had forgotten about her. She had to get back home. The Elders weren't going to help people away from the flood. She would have to do it herself, and she would start with Kim and Toby.

The rain pounded down. The churchyard path had become a tiny stream gushing down towards the gate. Lightning split the sky again, giving the churchyard one second of complete brightness. Laney ducked behind a headstone, afraid of who might see her in the sudden glare of light. Darkness fell again and she carried on crawling. A black cat ran in front of her. It stopped for a second, fixing its green eyes on her.

"Dizzy?" Laney was sure she recognised Claudia's favourite cat.

"Run, Laney!" Claudia hissed, darting past her. "Stingwood's hunting for you."

Laney sprang up and ran. She saw a bulky figure waiting by the gate at the far side of the churchyard and ran the other way. Reaching the wall, she pulled herself up and scrambled over. She was in human form, she suddenly realised. She didn't even know when her wings had disappeared. Her arms smarted from where she'd grazed them against the wall, but she carried on running, down the street and along the side alley by her house.

She pulled down the handle of the back door and almost fell inside. The bright light of the kitchen made it hard to see.

"Laney!" Kim stood holding Toby in her arms. "Thank goodness you're back. I've never seen rain like it. They're saying on the radio that there might be flash floods."

"Where's Dad? Is he back?"

"No. He left a phone message for me when I was making Toby's dinner. He and Simon are stuck on the main road out of town. The van broke down and Simon's gone to fetch a mechanic. I've tried ringing back but I'm not getting any answer. They probably don't know what's going on in Skellmore at all." She hugged Toby tighter.

"Mummy?" said Toby sleepily.

"It's all right, darling." Kim stroked his hair.

"Let's leave now, in the car," said Laney. "Let's get right out of Skellmore."

CHAPTER 25

Kim came back downstairs with a bag full of Toby's things. "OK, we can manage without everything else. Let's go."

Laney stood in the sitting room, looking round the edge of the curtain. She'd been expecting to see Mr Stingwood, or one of the other Elders, striding up the road to their front door. Jessie had tried to convince them that she'd caused the river to burst its banks and she was sure a lot of them had believed it.

The back door banged and Fletcher and Claudia ran through from the kitchen, dripping wet. "We didn't know if you'd made it back here," said Claudia. "It's crazy out there and—"

"Yeah, we've decided to leave in the car," said Laney, with a warning look towards Kim. "Better to go now."

"Better to stay here," said Fletcher quietly. "The High Street's now underwater. At least here you're part of the way up a hill. There's a chance the water won't reach you."

Kim turned white. "But if it gets worse we'll be cut off."

"Mummy?" Toby, dressed in red firemen pyjamas, bumped down the stairs on his bottom one step at a time. "Where tiger?"

"There's a tiger toy in the kitchen," said Fletcher.

Toby reached the bottom stair and toddled away

to find his tiger.

"It's his new favourite bedtime toy." Kim rested a hand on her forehead. "I just can't believe it – we've never had a flood around here before. Do your parents know that you're all right?"

"Don't worry about that," said Fletcher.

"All right, I'm going to try your dad's phone one more time, Laney." Kim went back upstairs.

As soon as she'd gone, Laney rounded on the others. "I have to get her and Toby out of here. If the High Street's blocked then we'll have to fly."

"But the faerie world—" said Claudia.

"Stuff the faerie world!" said Laney.

"No, Laney, wait," Claudia insisted. "Faeries have stayed secret for hundreds and hundreds of years. You can't just... I don't believe it, I sound like my mum!"

"I know you want your family to be safe," said Fletcher. "But what about the other humans living here? You won't be able to carry everybody to safety. You can't put yourself in danger just because you think the flood is your fault."

Tears filled Laney's eyes and she turned back to the window. "It is my stinking fault! I *gave* the mirror to the Shadow with all the Mist tribe power inside it. So, really, Jessie's right about everything!" She stared up at the storm clouds still pouring grey water over the village. She wasn't going to cry. It wouldn't help anyone.

Another bolt of lightning split the sky, followed by a boom of thunder. Laney closed her eyes for a second. She could still see the shape of the lightning on the inside of her eyelids. One jagged line at the top split into three pathways that split even further at the bottom, like the shape of an upside-down tree. It was almost pretty.

It had been raining for ages. How could the storm keep on going and going like this? How was there enough water in the sky for it to keep gushing down?

Her eyes snapped open.

There was *one* way the Shadow could make sure the storm didn't stop – one way he could make sure the rain kept on pouring. Now that she'd touched the mirror and felt its power it all made sense.

"What is it?" said Claudia. "You've suddenly gone all buzzy."

"How do you know?" said Fletcher.

"Greytails are very sensitive to changes of mood," said Claudia in a dignified tone.

Fletcher coughed in a way that sounded a bit like "As sensitive as my armpit", but Claudia ignored him.

"Listen!" Laney told them. "The Shadow is using the Crystal Mirror to cause the flood, right? So he must have taken it up there inside the clouds, otherwise the rain wouldn't keep going for this long."

"Laney?" Kim called. "I've just had a message from Tracey Mottle. She says the flood's reached window height on the High Street and there's water creeping up Beacon Way. That means the flood could be here in minutes. Check all the windows and doors are shut."

"OK," Laney called back.

"So what are we supposed to do?" hissed Claudia. "Fly up to certain death in the middle of a cloud? No thanks!"

"If we don't get the mirror back, he'll be able to drown the countryside any time he wants," said Fletcher. "People die in floods all the time. Their cars get washed away or they get hurt by the wreckage that's loose in the floodwater."

Laney shivered. She couldn't stop thinking of her dad. He can fly, she told herself, and maybe the flood wouldn't get as far as the road to town.

"Just a second." Fletcher ran upstairs and returned a moment later. "I've told Kim we're checking on the neighbours to see if anyone needs help. That'll stop her worrying about where we are."

Laney raced to the back door, which was slightly open, showing a tiny glimpse of the darkness outside.

"I still think this is a crazy idea," said Claudia. "Even if we find the Shadow, how are we going to take the mirror from someone that powerful? Laney? What's the matter?"

Laney stopped dead with her hand on the back door. "Where's Toby?"

The kitchen was empty. The living room was empty too.

"He didn't go back upstairs," said Claudia. "I would have seen him."

They all looked at the back door standing ajar.

A small furry tiger lay on the kitchen table. "He came in here to get that toy," said Fletcher.

Laney spun round, searching behind the door, under the kitchen table and behind the sitting room sofa – anywhere she could think of. She felt as if a giant hand was squeezing her ribcage.

"Stop a minute!" Fletcher grabbed her arm. "Are we sure he went outside? Claudia?"

Claudia closed her eyes. "He's definitely not in the house. I'd be able to sense him through sound or smell."

Laney ran out of the back door. "Toby!" A rushing, gurgling sound came from the front of the house. She ran down the side alley just as a cascade of water washed down Oldwing Rise from the direction of the stream at the end of the street.

Something small and red moved by the front wall. Toby, in his firemen pyjamas, opened the gate and pushed himself through on his ride-on car. He stopped to look at the torrent gushing down the middle of the road.

Laney tore down the front path just as Toby got off the little plastic car and crouched down by the edge of the road. The flood rose, pouring on to the pavement and surging into the front garden. Toby reached out for something that was sweeping past him in the water. He wobbled and fell in.

Laney dived towards him but he was swept away down the road. She tried to yell but her face went under the water. Surrounded by the flood, her Mist energy fizzed through every cell of her body. She seized power from the water and transformed. Wings burst from her shoulders and she soared into the air.

Claudia and Fletcher were flying over the rooftops at high speed. "He's nearly got to the street corner!" Claudia shouted. "And the flood that's rising up Beacon Way has joined up with water running down the main road from Skellmore Edge. If he falls into that he could get sucked under."

Beneath the roar of the water, Laney could hear Toby crying. She flew low over the flood and saw a small face and arms with red pyjama sleeves swirling in the water.

Fletcher flew down. "Catch hold of the tree, Toby!" He pointed at a beech tree that bent its branches over the water for the little boy to catch hold of.

But Toby missed the tree and was swept on, still crying. His little face looked up for one last moment as he reached the corner of Beacon Way and went under. Laney plunged into the flood after him. She swam hard, slipping round sunken garden furniture and other rubbish that had been carried along by the torrent. She found Toby, grabbed hold of him and held him tight. Together they broke through the surface of the water, rising up into the warm night air.

"Toby, are you all right?" Laney gasped.

Toby coughed and clasped his little arms round her neck. "Laney got wings!"

"You scared me," said Laney. "Don't do that! Stay inside with Mummy." She flew up over the rooftops, avoiding the windows of Oldwing Rise and any humans that might be watching.

"I rescued the little car." Fletcher flew past with the ride-on car under one arm. "Claudia's on the ground. Her wings got too wet to fly."

Laney hugged Toby tighter as they flew downwards. Lightning cracked the sky and the thunder roared. Toby whimpered, but she shushed him gently.

"Laney, look," said Fletcher, pointing skywards. In the thickest part of the storm clouds, red lights flickered.

"That's where he is," whispered Laney. "That's where he's holding the mirror." Looking at Fletcher's face she could see he thought the same.

They swooped down to Laney's back garden where Claudia was waiting. "My wings gave out." A pair of bedraggled wings dripped behind her shoulders.

Laney flew to the ground and handed Toby to Claudia. "Stay here and look after them for me, please."

Claudia hugged Toby. "Are you still going up there? Laney...what if it's impossible?"

"He's not going to stop until he's drowned the whole place," said Laney. "Until everything and everyone gets swept away."

"Here – you'd better have this." Claudia set Toby down for a moment. She unfastened a thin black cord from around her neck. It had something pointed and pearly-white dangling from it. "It's a wolf's tooth. It's supposed to help with speed and stamina."

"Thanks." Laney put it on as Claudia hurried inside with Toby and shut the door.

Laney flew upwards with Fletcher beside her. They headed straight for the thickest part of the storm clouds. Below, Skellmore lay under a shifting mass of water. People stood at their upstairs windows, watching the flood rise. The grey water swept a tide of junk along with it. Plastic bottles, tree branches and a dustbin floated by. On the High Street, only the roofs of the parked cars could be seen above the water.

Laney rose into the night sky. She knew she had to climb quickly, before the dread of what she had to do caught hold. The wind and rain battered her, making it hard to fly in a straight line.

"The higher we go, the thinner the air will be," shouted Fletcher. "It might get hard to breathe."

Laney watched the world below shrinking. The Skellmore streetlights were now tiny orange pinpricks. She spread her wings and flew harder. Up here the rain was half frozen. It stung her arms and legs. Fletcher puffed beside her, his face slightly blue.

"Go back! It's OK," she told him.

Fletcher didn't answer. He pointed.

Red lightning flickered round the inside of the cloud above. Fear spread through Laney like a poison. She had thought she could do this. She had planned to be brave.

"Hey!" Fletcher coughed. He cleared his throat. "Hey!"

"What are you doing?" said Laney.

Fletcher swept past her and the cloud swallowed him up. "Hey!" he shouted. "Where are you, you monster?"

Laney's heart raced. He couldn't go in there. He didn't have water wings like she did, and when the Shadow saw him... She shot after him. The rain cloud surrounded her and red lightning crackled through the greyness.

A dark figure loomed out of the cloud vapour. In one black-gloved hand he held the Crystal Mirror and in the other he held Fletcher by the throat.

Laney could see Fletcher's eyes and she understood. She should get the mirror now, before the Shadow saw her. She stretched out her hands and with all the Mist power she could gather, she commanded the cloud water to seize the mirror and carry it to her.

The Crystal Mirror spun free from the Shadow's hand and floated through the fog.

The Shadow turned with a furious cry. He let go of Fletcher, who collapsed, falling through the cloud and disappearing. Laney caught hold of the round mirror and threw herself sideways, just as the Shadow stretched out his hand and let loose his red lightning.

CHAPTER 26

Laney's arm filled with pain and she knew the lightning must have hit her. She hugged the mirror to her chest as she fell. Above, a great black shape opened his wings and plunged after her.

Skellmore rushed closer. She knew she should open her wings to slow her fall, but they wouldn't unfold. It doesn't matter, she told herself. I rescued the mirror and took its power away from the Shadow, and that's what I meant to do. Her head was spinning. Weariness spread outwards from her wound like a poison, travelling up her arm into her shoulder and neck.

She carried on falling. She could see the High Street below her and the lights of the houses. The park's oak tree stood in a lake of water, except for the green circle of the faerie ring. The floodwater swirled round the ring without touching it. Voices sang to Laney. She shouldn't be afraid, they said; the ring would catch her when she fell.

"Laney!" Fletcher yelled from a nearby roof. "You're going to land too close to the ring."

Laney unfolded her wings and struggled to change direction but the mirror dragged her downwards. She couldn't move her wounded arm at all now and her wings hardly worked. But the darkness coming from her wound felt gentle now, like soft snow. She closed her eyes.

"Laney!" Fletcher's voice sounded fainter.

She felt a rough jolt and opened her eyes. The Shadow grasped the mirror, his dark hood nearly touching her face. "Give it to me!"

"No!" Laney could feel the power of the faerie ring now. A vortex of air sucked her downwards and sweet voices sang, inviting her to a new home beyond the ring.

The Shadow felt it too. He wrenched the mirror out of Laney's hands, but a gust of wind pushed him sideways and knocked the mirror away. Seeing the mirror falling finally woke Laney up. She spread her wings and fought against the swirling pull of the ring. The Shadow struggled against it too and broke free, only to fall into the floodwater.

Laney dragged herself away from the ring. She hit the icy water and sank instantly. The water trembled around her, full of unnatural power. If she could just get to the mirror first, she could send the flood away into the ground. She could save Skellmore.

She groped through the murky water until she saw a glimmer of brightness lying on the bottom – the reflection that looked like a thousand stars. She took hold of the mirror and with all the strength she had left she silently commanded the flood to leave – to sink back into the earth where it belonged.

Her wound throbbed. She felt the flood churn around her and finally the darkness inside her grew so strong that she couldn't stay conscious any more.

When she came round she was lying halfway down Gnarlwood Lane with her feet propped up against a tree and mud in her hair.

Fletcher looked down, his dark fringe hanging over one eye. "She's waking up."

"Let her rest a little," said a quiet voice that Laney knew at once belonged to Gwen.

She blinked. The sky above her was scattered with stars. That meant the storm clouds were gone. Realising her hands were empty, she panicked and tried to sit up. "Where's the mirror? Have we got it?"

Gwen smiled. "Yes, we have the Crystal Mirror. You were holding it when we found you, and the flood's going down too. So just lie still for a minute. You were out for quite a while."

"Gwen did a healing spell on you using willow bark and skullcap leaves," said Fletcher. "It was pretty amazing. You had loads of cuts and they all just vanished."

Gwen turned away and began whispering to something in the palm of her hand. A crowd of little brown dots hovered in the air for a moment and then drifted away.

"Is that seed magic?" said Fletcher. "I've never

seen any done before."

Gwen tucked her white hair under the edges of her purple rain hat. "It is indeed seed magic, Fletcher Thornbeam."

Laney could tell that Fletcher was hoping Gwen would explain a bit more, but she just smiled reassuringly. "Would you like a cookie?" She produced a small flowery tin from her pocket and offered it to them.

"Yes, please. I'm hungry." Laney pulled herself up, trying to ignore the way her head was spinning. She took a bite from the cookie, noticing that the mirror lay a little distance away on the ground. Even smeared with mud it still gave out a feeling of immense power. "What happened to the Shadow?"

"I saw him fall into the water," said Fletcher. "I flew above the flood and tried to see whether he was washed away from here, but I didn't see him again."

"The Shadow will not have left forever," said Gwen. "I suspect after tonight he will be drained of power and won't be able to make more trouble for us straight away. But we cannot be too careful – we must hide the Myrical immediately."

"I wish I'd never found it!" said Laney. "That's what he wanted all the time."

"It doesn't matter now. You got it back and you were incredibly brave to do so," Gwen told her.

With a rustle of wings, Claudia flew down beside them. "Laney! You're OK! I've been looking everywhere for you. Gwen! You're back!"

"I flew back as soon as I heard reports of the flood on the television." Gwen gracefully caught the handful of seeds as they returned from wherever they'd been. She listened to them for a moment and then put them in her pocket.

"How are Kim and Toby?" Laney asked Claudia urgently.

"They're fine. I stayed with them until the flood went down," said Claudia. "The water came right through the front door, but we were OK upstairs. Then your dad came back. He'd obviously heard about the flood while he was waiting for his van to be fixed. He had to make up a story to tell your stepmum about how he managed to get back here without driving."

Laney sighed with relief. "They're all safe."

"They'll be even safer once this Myrical is hidden." Gwen picked up the Crystal Mirror. "Have you got enough strength to fly, Laney?"

"I think so." Laney looked down at her sodden jeans and T-shirt. "I just need some wings."

"That's the easy part, my dear." Gwen touched Laney's shoulders and her wings sprouted.

A pale morning glow appeared in the east as they flew away from Skellmore. Sunrise wouldn't be long now, Laney thought. She needed sleep.

Too tired to talk, Laney, Claudia and Fletcher followed Gwen across the dark fields. They skirted round the edge of Hobbin Forest and landed near the river. On a nearby hilltop a huge round stone with a hole in its centre stood outlined against the lightening sky. Laney could feel the power coming from the faerie ring that lay behind them near the riverbank.

"Why have we come to Mencladden Hill?" said Claudia.

"If we hide the mirror like a human would – bury it or lock it away – the Shadow will find it," said Gwen. "He's already proved that he wants to use its power. But if we lock the Myrical away inside Time itself, then nobody will be able to touch it."

"Not ever?" Laney didn't know how she felt about never seeing the Crystal Mirror again.

"The spell lasts for a year and a day, and it can only be performed at sunrise, so we need to hurry." Gwen walked up the hillside towards the standing stone with the mirror in both hands.

"Can't we just fly up there?" said Claudia, yawning.

"Not this time," Gwen called back. "We don't want to upset the vibrations in the air, especially after the storm last night. This is a delicate spell we're going to perform and the Mencladden Stone is an unusual place."

Laney hurried to keep up, surprised at how fast Gwen was climbing. "What do we have to do?"

"It's what *you* have to do," said Gwen. "Only someone that belongs to the Myrical's tribe can perform the spell, so in this case it has to be you. It's quite easy. You simply pass the mirror through the stone."

"*Through* the stone?" Claudia's eyes popped. "That's some kind of magic."

"She means through the hole in the middle," said Fletcher drily.

"Oh! I knew that," said Claudia.

When they reached the top, the landscape was turning from black to grey, and a golden spot gleamed in one corner of the sky where the sun was about to rise. The Mencladden Stone towered over them. Laney wondered why she'd never noticed before that the outside of the stone was perfectly round while the hole in the middle was oval. It reminded her of a cat's eye.

"We only have a few minutes." Gwen straightened her purple hat. "Quickly, Laney. Stand behind the stone so that you can see the sun as soon as it peeps over the horizon. You must be standing in exactly the right place. Then, when you see those first rays, put the mirror right through the hole."

Laney shifted sideways until she could see the

glow in the sky where the sun was about to appear. She leaned on the weather-worn stone to steady herself. It had been a very long night.

Fletcher handed her the mirror. "Shall I stand on the other side and take the mirror when she's passed it through?" he asked Gwen.

"If all goes well there will be no need," said Gwen.

"Sorry?" Fletcher looked confused.

"She said there will be *no need*," said Claudia, not very helpfully.

Laney took a slow breath to try to calm her racing heartbeat. What if she did this wrong? What if she didn't put the mirror through at the right moment? "What else do I need to do, Gwen?"

"Just watch for the sunrise," said Gwen.

Silence settled over the hilltop and colour gradually seeped into the grass and trees and sky. When the curved edge of the sun rose it looked like liquid gold. The mirror reflected those first rays of sunlight in its crystal surface a thousand times over.

"Now, Laney!" Gwen said.

Laney lifted the heavy mirror in both hands and tilted it to fit into the hole in the stone. Carefully she posted it through, but as the mirror reached halfway it stopped and stayed stuck in mid-air.

"Go on," said Claudia. "Put it all the way through."

"I can't!" Laney shoved harder. "It won't go." She looked at Gwen for help, but Gwen said nothing.

"Here, I'll do it." Fletcher strode forwards.

"It has to be someone from the Mist tribe," said Gwen. "Laney, you *must* make it pass through, my dear. This is our best chance to keep the mirror safe."

Laney pushed with all her strength, throwing her whole weight against the Crystal Mirror, which was shining brighter and brighter in the growing sunlight. For a few seconds she stayed like that, pushing against something that hung in mid-air inside the hole.

Her hand throbbed painfully and a bright-red mark blossomed on her middle finger. Then a tall flame burst from the top of the Mencladden Stone and blazed brightly for a few seconds before flickering out. At the same time, the mirror slid the rest of the way through the gap and vanished completely as if it had never existed.

With nothing left to push against, Laney fell over on to her knees, clutching her sore finger and feeling sad that the Myrical was gone.

CHAPTER
27

"Blimey! That was mad." Claudia offered Laney a hand and pulled her up. "You didn't say there would be fire as well."

"I wasn't expecting the flame." Gwen clasped her thin arms together and suddenly she looked very old.

"My finger really hurts." Laney examined the bright-red mark.

"Are you burned?" Fletcher strode forwards to look at her hand.

"Yes! No! I mean that flame just then didn't touch me. This is a burn I got last week, but it had healed up," said Laney. "Was the spell meant to do that?"

"I don't believe so, but I've only seen the spell performed once before and that wasn't with a Myrical," said Gwen. "The important thing is that it worked. There will be no way to reach the Crystal Mirror until a year and a day has passed." She began to walk slowly back down the hill.

"So what do we do now?" Laney flew after her. "We just wait for a year and a day and then get it back out again?"

Gwen looked at her sadly. "I haven't told you why I went away, have I?"

"Did you go to see some other Elders?" said Fletcher.

"Yes, I went north to the Lostbryn Hills where large numbers of the Thorn and Kestrel tribes still live." Gwen stopped walking and looked at the three of them. "I'm afraid you will find it harder to remain friends in the days to come. Tribal wounds have always taken a long time to heal, and there are those who will take pleasure in blaming the other side for what has happened tonight."

Laney swallowed. "You mean the tribes still won't believe that there was a Shadow faerie? They won't understand that he caused the flood?"

Gwen sighed. "They didn't see him and they always find it hard to believe what they cannot see. They will blame each other, starting with the Mist tribe because of their power over water, and those who want to bridge the divide will be shouted down once more."

"We can tell them what really happened," said Fletcher. "We all saw the Shadow."

Gwen looked at him for a moment. A small red poppy uncurled from the ground and bent lovingly against her shoe. "You mustn't do that. At least for now."

She walked on a little. "I went north to find out everything I could about this Shadow and what he wants. You see, the five Myricals were hidden from an enemy called the Great Shadow many years ago. In the end, the Great Shadow was beaten, but the sacred Myricals stayed hidden. The forgotten faerie lore of the north says that at least three of them were concealed in the same area. You've found one – there may be more nearby. This new Shadow with his dark power must *not* find them."

"But it would be great if they were nearby!" said Fletcher. "I'd love to find the Wildwood Arrow…"

"The Shadow will be looking for them, won't he?" said Laney.

"I believe he will. The Myricals contain immense power and until we know who the Shadow is, it would be better not to mention what you've seen to anyone," said Gwen. "Promise me you'll keep this to yourselves for the time being."

"I promise," said Fletcher.

"And me," said Laney.

"I wasn't planning on sharing it," said Claudia. "But if I wanted to tell the whole world I'd talk to Mrs Mottle."

As Laney walked back through Skellmore with Claudia and Fletcher, she couldn't believe how much damage the flood had done. The water had vanished, but it had left tonnes of mud and rubbish behind. An upside-down armchair rested in the middle of the High Street where it had been dumped by the receding water. A pair of slippers lay on top of the churchyard wall. People were up and about, throwing out soaked carpets and rescuing belongings from the muck.

"I haven't been so worried since we had those storms in 1997," Laney heard Mrs Mottle say to her next-door neighbour. "I was glad I had Craig to carry everything upstairs. He did a brilliant job. And did you see all that lightning? Some of it actually looked red. I rang up the television station this morning and they're sending someone over later to do an interview. I must go and find something nice to wear."

Claudia rolled her eyes. "Can you imagine her on TV?" she muttered.

"I just hope she doesn't go on about the red lightning," said Laney.

Fletcher hurried back towards Gnarlwood Lane, telling them he had to go and check on his family.

Laney and Claudia walked on up Beacon Way. As they passed The Cattery, the spiny house on the corner snarled miserably as if it hated being surrounded by mud.

"I bet my mum and dad and Tom found somewhere nice and dry to go," said Claudia as they rounded the corner into Oldwing Rise. "We all hate the rain."

"But you still came with me last night," said Laney. "And you looked after Kim and Toby. I owe you one." She staggered backwards suddenly, as someone grabbed her arm. "What are you…"

Jessie stood there, her eyes burning. "You did

this! And the Mist tribe spent all night trying to get rid of the flood, while you were hanging out with a Greytail."

For a second Laney wished she could tell Jessie what really happened. She would have loved to see the look on Jessie's face after telling her that she, Laney Rivers, had held the treasured Mist Myrical. But she had promised Gwen to keep everything secret.

"Which is it?" she snapped at Jessie. "First you tell me I don't have enough power to be in your tribe. Then you say I've made the storm that flooded the whole village. You need to work out which story you actually believe, because right now nothing you say sounds like the truth."

Jessie's mouth dropped open.

"And has anyone told you that mud really isn't your best look?" said Claudia, eyeing Jessie's filthy jeans.

"That told her," said Laney as they walked away.

Claudia stopped at the Riverses' front gate. Laney saw Toby waving at her from an upstairs window and she waved back.

"Last night – all that water," Claudia shuddered. "You saved Skellmore. Seriously, if there *is* anything in all that red moon stuff – and I don't really believe in it – then maybe it's a good thing you Awakened on that day."

Faerie
TRIBES

"Thanks." Laney didn't really know what else to say.

"But no more flying through storms, OK? It really freaked me out."

"No more storm flying," said Laney, opening the gate and walking down the path. "Not until next time anyway!"

As Claudia left, Laney glanced up at the dappled blue light playing across the cottage walls. She went inside. The sitting room carpet squelched under her feet and patches of mud decorated the sofa. She sighed. There was a lot to do.

"I know it looks bad." Her dad leaned against the doorway. "But it's only furniture. It can all be replaced." He smiled, although his eyes still looked serious. "The storm was bad last night."

"Some of the tribes fought each other. Have they always done that?" asked Laney, thinking of what had happened in the churchyard.

"Always. They can't help themselves," her dad said bitterly. "And each tribe is as bad as the other."

Laney turned away. "I should go and help Kim." She swept a hand above the damp armchair and a scattering of water drops rose up from the cushions.

Her dad coughed. "Laney? Your mum…" he said quietly. "She was a faerie too. I expect you guessed that already."

258

Laney turned towards him eagerly. "I hoped she was…"

"And when she died…I didn't want to have anything to do with the faerie world any more. I'm sorry if I've made all of this harder for you."

"It's all right, Dad." She met his eyes. Somehow she didn't mind them being gold-ringed any more.

"When all of this has died down, I'll go to see the other members of the Mist tribe to make sure they give you all the basic Mist power training."

"But Miss Reed said I wouldn't be allowed."

"Don't worry about Miss Reed. She's not a Mist tribe Elder. I know she'd like to step into Arthur Puddlewick's shoes, but the rest of the tribe will never choose her and I hear she failed to hold back the flood last night." He shook his head. "Trust me, Laney. The Mist tribe members won't put her in charge. I'll talk to them and make sure you get your training."

"Thanks, Dad!" Laney beamed.

"It will help you control your powers." He smiled a little. "We can't have you breaking any more water pipes at school, can we?"

"Laney, are you back?" Kim came downstairs and hugged her tightly. "Claudia said you were helping the neighbours last night. Is everyone all right?"

"I think so." Laney hugged her back. "There's a lot of clearing up to do though. The whole village is such a mess."

"Let's start by getting rid of this thing." Laney's dad prodded the water-laden carpet with his toe. "It's past saving."

"Laney!" Toby grinned from the top of the stairs. "Wings, Laney!"

"Toby!" Laney smiled back, happy to see him safe. She sneaked a look at Kim, who didn't seem surprised that Toby was talking about wings. It was just toddler talk after all.

An engine rumbled outside. "That'll be Simon," said Mr Rivers. "At least the van must be fixed."

A door slammed and Simon appeared, grinning. "I heard how bad it was on the radio, but the water's actually gone down really quickly." He held out some paper parcels. "I brought chips from the chip shop in town to help make the clear-up easier."

CHAPTER 28

Laney couldn't sleep that night. At first she thought it was because she didn't want to dream, but she knew the Crystal Mirror was out of reach. There would be no more dreams about it. There was something else.

She pulled back the curtain and looked up at the three-quarters moon. Her middle finger throbbed where it had been burned, making her think of her birthday and everything that had happened since. Without hesitating, she opened the window, changed into faerie form and flew out over Oldwing Rise. She circled around the edge of Skellmore and landed in Gnarlwood Lane in front of Gwen's gate. One of the gigantic trumpet-shaped flowers quivered and a line of greenish smoke trailed up into the night.

Gwen opened her front door wearing a small, cream-coloured hat. "Hello, Laney. I've been expecting you."

Laney followed her in and they sat down in the plant house. A bunch of sprites hung from the end of a branch above them, casting a dappled pink and white light over the room.

"Are they asleep?" asked Laney, peering at them.

"Yes, but they never sleep for very long," said Gwen. "You came to ask me something, didn't you?"

Laney rubbed the arm of the bench with one

finger. "How do you know – is it some kind of Thorn power?"

"No, it's because I'm old and because I know you, Laney Rivers. You were never going to be satisfied with half an answer." Gwen smiled and the lines on her face wrinkled. "What is it you want to know?"

Laney took a deep breath. "What is the prophecy about the red moon? I mean, what does it actually say?"

"It says this," said Gwen, before reciting slowly: "*Born under a Wolf Moon, the Child of Aether joins together powers far apart. He binds the opposites and drives a splinter through the faerie ring's heart.*"

Laney paused, trying to take this in. "The Child of Aether? What does that mean?"

"No one knows for sure."

"But the tribes think that person – the Child of Aether – will be dangerous?"

"Some of them do. But no one knows for sure what the prophecy means or whether the faerie it refers to has even been born yet." Gwen rose from the bench. "Now, let me get you some Thorn elixir. After the flood and the chaos, I think we could both do with some. And maybe some chocolate cookies?"

"Yes, please." Laney sat still as Gwen went to the kitchen. She touched the burn mark on her finger, which was still as red and sore as it had been at the Mencladden Stone. She didn't know why it had suddenly flared up again on the hill that morning. Her finger certainly hadn't touched the flame that time.

The Child of Aether joins together powers far apart. That sounded like some kind of spell.

He binds the opposites and drives a splinter through the faerie ring's heart. Well, she wasn't a *he*, so how could the prophecy be about her?

Deciding it was too confusing to think about any more, she followed Gwen to the kitchen to get her chocolate cookies and elixir.

Helping her dad and Kim with the clear-up took all of Laney's time for a few days. By Saturday the house looked almost back to normal, except for the bare floors. Laney noticed thick fog hanging over Skellmore Edge and wondered if the faeries had made it. She shivered and went back to hanging out the sofa cushions. She was glad she didn't have to go up there and be grilled for answers this time.

Claudia and Fletcher came down the lane that afternoon.

"Go and have some fun," Kim told her. "This is your summer holiday and you need some time off. While you're out can you get me some milk from the shop?"

"OK." Laney hurried through the gate.

"You didn't come to listen to the Faerie Meet this morning," said Fletcher as soon as they were out of earshot.

"It was great," said Claudia. "The tribes started arguing and Gwen gave them a complete telling-off. She went on about how loads of them just left Skellmore during the flood without staying to help the humans or support the Mist tribe as they fought the water. She said she was really ashamed of them and they all went dead quiet."

"Good for Gwen," said Laney.

"So they sort of made up after that," said Claudia. "And Gwen told them blaming you for the flood was ridiculous, and she said lots of the Mists had done a good job in helping the water go down quickly."

"So she kept the news about the Myricals completely secret?" said Laney.

"She didn't mention them at all," said Claudia. "So at least everything is back to normal."

"What about Mr Stingwood?" said Laney. "He doesn't seem like the type to let things go." She paused. "Do you remember when we were in the churchyard just as the flood started and someone cast a spell on him? I've been thinking about it for days. He was tangled up in a vine, so it must have been another Thorn faerie that did it."

Fletcher grinned. "Yeah, that was me!"

"Fletcher! I never thought you'd do that!" said Laney.

Fletcher dug his hands into his pockets. "Well, I thought he was about to do something nasty with that walking stick. Don't tell anyone, OK? He would really have it in for me if he knew."

They rounded the corner and went down the footpath towards the Mistray river. Although the flood had retreated from the village, the river was still three times wider than normal. Bits of higher ground poked out of the water like tiny islands.

"There's no one around," said Claudia. "Let's do some flying!"

"It's the middle of the day," said Fletcher.

Laney closed her eyes and changed to faerie form. "Race you!" She took off, skimming just above the river.

"Cheat!" called Fletcher, spreading his wings and chasing.

They circled over the water until Laney landed on a little island that was hidden under the shade of a tree.

"It's weird to think that this was a disaster zone a few days ago, all because of the Crystal Mirror," said Claudia. "They're blaming it all on freak storms on the TV. Do you think one day the humans will notice what's going on?"

Laney shook her head. "They'll never notice."

"Our world will stay secret," said Fletcher. "As long as you can stop breaking water pipes at school, Laney."

Laney smiled, watching a dragonfly dip over the river. This was a good time to tell them her plan. "I've been thinking since the night of the storm… I think we should start looking for the other Myricals."

"What? We'll end up getting killed," said Claudia.

"I know it's dangerous, but we're the only ones who can do it," Laney told her. "Nobody except Gwen knows what the Shadow did or how we found the Crystal Mirror. None of them would want to believe it anyway."

"And Gwen told us it wasn't safe to tell anyone else," said Fletcher. "Come on, don't tell me you wouldn't like to find the Greytail Myrical!"

"OK, maybe I would," said Claudia. "But where would we look for it?"

"I don't know," said Laney.

"The Wildwood Arrow, the Vial of the Four Winds, the Sparkstone and the White Wolf Statue," said Claudia thoughtfully. "They're all out there somewhere."

"The Shadow will be searching too." Fletcher folded his arms. "It won't be easy."

"That's why we need to get started," said Laney. "I think we should get ready, learn to fly better and learn how to fight back as well."

"We should be better prepared for next time," Fletcher agreed.

"But we need some chill time this summer too, right?" Claudia raised her eyebrows. "It all sounds like a lot of work."

Fletcher took off and hovered over the river. "I don't think I'll need any flying lessons though. It's not like I'm a slowcoach Mist faerie!"

"The cheek! I'll get you for that!" Laney pointed at the river below, raising a jet of water to drench him. He dodged sideways and she dived after him, arching her wings as she soared into the pale-blue sky.